WINTER OF THE OWL

Other APPLE PAPERBACKS you will want to read:

WINTER OF THE OWL

by

June Andrea Hanson

AN
APPLE
PAPERBACK

SCHOLASTIC BOOK SERVICES
New York Toronto London Auckland Sydney Tokyo

This one is for Nathan Obawole

ISBN 0-590-32775-5

12 11 10 9 8 7 6 5 4 3 2 1   1   3 4 5 6 7/8

Contents

It Starts with a Thud

"Forget it. If I'm going to have to put up with some Indian who will be more trouble than help, just forget it. I'll handle the feeding alone. Every bit of it, including those fifty head you bought in the fall so we'd have to feed them through the winter." Grandpa's forehead wrinkles were deep gulleys above the frost in his eyebrows. His weathered cheeks were red with cold and anger.

"Oh, Henry, can't you understand?" Daddy shouted, steaming up his wire-rimmed glasses so that he couldn't see. He wiped at them with his wool glove as he continued: "I'm trying to make this ranch work. I've got everything staked on it. I'm not trying to aggravate you. I'm getting help out here because *you* say you need it."

"Talk about aggravation *now*, but you never talked to me about how much feed we had before you went out and bought those cows. No, it ain't just that you made it too much work for me and Marie to handle alone . . . feeding a herd that big, just the two of us. . . ." Grandpa shook his head and gave a snort. "No, that ain't the half of it!"

"Look, I'm getting someone who *will* help. This man's a good worker. He was doing sugar-beet work on one of the farms in the Yellowstone Valley. Now that's over, so he's available. He is a good worker and he needs the job. I don't see why you have to make such a big fuss." Daddy turned his back on Grandpa and walked toward the barn. I quickly pulled myself into the corner of a horse stall, deeper into the darkness and shadows where they couldn't see me.

"Why do I have to make such a big fuss?" Grandpa spit out across the snow between them. "I'll tell you why . . . because you've made such a mess of things. Now that you've stuck in those 'bargain cows,' as you call them, we don't have enough hay to get through even an easy winter. Just take a look around you! It's only the middle of December and you can't see the scrub sage anymore. We've had two feet of snow on the ground since Thanksgiving, and this part of Montana ain't known for its balmy Januarys. I've been feeding and chopping ice in the water holes every day for the last three weeks. Well, I can't do the work alone . . . and if we don't have enough feed, I won't even be able to do it *with* help. Then we'll see what a bargain those cows are when you have to buy hay trucked in from the Lord-knows-where, if you can get any at all." Grandpa hissed and took a swinging kick at a hunk of snow, sending out a spray of it that spattered on Daddy's dark overcoat.

"Listen here, Henry," Daddy shouted, "If you're so worried about having enough hay, I mean if we really do stand a chance of running short, then you darned well better get rid of those extra horses you've been running out here free of charge. They're surely no asset. Those two mares are impossible to ride, so skittish and nuts that we can't even offer them to the extra help at branding roundup . . . and that colt hasn't been broken yet. Before I take any more abuse about buying cattle, which *are* an asset to the ranch, you better think about paying me fair pasturing price for those horses, including their winter feed, or get rid of them."

"No!" I gasped from my hiding place before I could stop myself. I stuffed my mitten into my mouth. No one had heard me.

3

"You . . ." Grandpa took a step toward Daddy. I thought he was going to hit him. I almost screamed. Then, just as he raised his fist, Grandpa spun around. He stood there, only a few yards away from the barn door, staring out through the corrals toward the big bluff across the river. His gloved fist was clenched and ready near his shoulder. I didn't dare move. I didn't dare breathe. No one spoke. Except for Daddy's breath, which rose out of his muffler and curled into the frozen air like a cloud of smoke, there was no movement. They looked like statues . . . until Grandpa slammed his fist into the side of the barn. A lone chicken that had been pecking at some spilled oats in a horse stall squawked in fright and flapped past me, half-flying, half-walking. I ducked to avoid her wings.

"OK! I'll sell off the horses at the January auction, but *you* won't see the money! I've been running this place, doing the work of two men . . . doing it for you and my daughter and my grandkids and getting durn little out of it myself . . . working like a dog for nothing, so whatever I get for those horses is mine!" Grandpa thumped the front of his mackinaw with his fist. "Mine, you hear?"

"It's not my fault you haven't made money," Daddy yelled back. "You've signed the lease every year, agreed to it. You've gotten your

4

money out of the deal, but I haven't always gotten mine. What about my share on that hay we sold off the bluestem meadow three years ago?" Daddy stopped and wiped at his glasses again. He took a deep breath. "Look, Henry. Let's try to make this work out. I'll get the hired man out here as soon as I can . . . maybe even by tomorrow. I'm going to head back to the depot now. I'll get there before dark. I can probably see him tonight. His name is Tom Yellowfeather. He's got a wife and a boy, so have the bunkhouse ready." Daddy didn't wait for Grandpa's reply. He started walking through the snow toward the house. I could hear it crunching beneath his rubber galoshes.

Grandpa moved slowly around the sled toward the barn. I pressed deeper into the corner and knelt down on my knees behind a broken bale of straw. As Grandpa's footsteps came closer to the barn door, I pulled my coat up around my ears and my scarf over my mouth and nose to cover my breath. I didn't want him to see me when he was this mad.

Grandpa stomped past me and headed for the stalls at the other end of the barn where the black team stood waiting to be unharnessed. From my darkened corner I could see his silhouette in the light from the window. At the entrance to the stall he stopped, took off his glove and reached into the pocket of his big mackinaw. He pulled out a wadded-up handkerchief, blew his nose furiously, and put the handkerchief back into his pocket. He glared at a water pail sitting on the floor in front of him, then kicked it so it clanged and rolled into the stall, making the horse jump.

"Hold still, you jackass!" Grandpa shouted as he stepped into the stall.

I quickly slid out from behind the straw bale and tiptoed out the door. Then I ran as fast as I could toward the house. I had to see Daddy before he left. I had to talk to him. It was so cold, my chest and throat were burning when I jumped up on the back porch and opened the door into the washroom. I didn't stop to hang up my coat or take off my boots. I lifted the heavy green curtain that was hung in the doorway to the kitchen to keep out the draft.

"Where's Daddy?" I asked.

Mom, Grandma and Greg all looked up at me at the same time.

"Who wants him?" Greg asked, grinning.

"The man in the moon, jerk," I answered.

"Don't talk to your brother like that! Honestly, I thought it would get better as you got older, but. . . ." Mom shook her head in disgust.

"Your father went upstairs to pack, Janey," Grandma said.

I was through the door and up the stairs before anyone had a chance to tell me I was tracking snow in the house.

Daddy was sitting on his bed, staring out the window. He didn't even seem to have heard me clomping up the stairs two at a time. I stopped before I entered the room. I hadn't thought of what I was going to say to him. How could I talk to him about the colt without letting him know I'd heard the fight, that I was eavesdropping. Maybe I should tell him. I didn't listen in on purpose. I was just getting that new halter out of the tack room when they started yelling at each other. I was afraid to leave. I would have, if I could have without them seeing me. I hated their dumb fights. They were always going at it about something. I guess the best thing to do was to start talking and take my chances.

"Why are you going back to the depot so early, Daddy?" I asked, breaking into the silence.

"I have to get out of here. It's going to snow," he said as he stuck his wool shirt into the old briefcase he used as a suitcase. He dropped his shaving kit on top of it and looked up at me over the rims of his glasses. He started to speak, stopped and turned toward the window again.

All you could see through the leaves of frost on the pane were the dark gray fenceposts stretched out over the prairie snow, growing smaller and

7

smaller until they became tiny burnt matchsticks and disappeared into the sky on the rim of the hill. Daddy stared at them for a long time.

"It's always something, always something. Can't get ahead for the life of me," he mumbled, shaking his head. "Here I own the prettiest spread in southeastern Montana . . . rich land, good water with the old Tongue River running right through it. It is all I ever wanted . . . along with my family, and I can't even enjoy it. I'll probably spend the rest of my life working for the railroad. Never be able to give up that depot agent job; I'll just keep pumping money in here. It's poor management, that's what's wrong. Now your grandfather wants a hired man for the winter. I'm going to have to take the money I planned to use to put in the electricity. They're supposed to get the wires out this far sometime in the spring."

Daddy sighed. "I know he's getting too old to do the work, but he's family. I can't fire him and get someone out here who *can* do the work. So I'm saddled with paying for two hands. I've got to get some relief."

Suddenly I had an idea! "Daddy, listen, I can help you. I could take the place of the summer hired help. Wouldn't that make it better? See, I could do the chores, milking and stuff, ride herd, that's no problem, and I could help with the hay-

ing. I know I could. I ran the stacker last summer. I know I could learn to mow. I'd just need
lessons on how to run the machinery. I can handle the team. I can drive the tractor. I could do
it, Daddy. That way you wouldn't have to pay
anybody. I'd work for you, for free . . . except
for. . . ."

"Wait a minute, young lady," Daddy said,
holding up his hand. "I appreciate your offer,
and I'm sure you could learn to do all those
things, but I know what you're leading up to.
You're going to ask me for that colt again, and
the answer is still no! We've more stock on the
ranch than we can feed now. We don't need any
more horses."

"But he's here. It isn't like getting another
horse."

"But not for long. I just told your grandfather
he has to sell the colt and the two mares. We
can't keep them through the winter, Janey. It
looks like it's going to be a rough one, and we're
already short of hay. I can't afford to run any su-
perfluous stock. You're only out here on occa-
sional weekends and during school vacations to
ride. Your own horse would be a luxury we can't
afford. Besides, this one isn't broken and it
doesn't have very promising breeding for a good
saddle horse. No, forget it. Forget the colt. If I
get straightened around financially so I can re-

tire from the railroad before I die, we'll move out here for good, and then you can have your own horse . . . a nice one that's been broken and proven already."

"I don't want a nice, proven horse. I want this colt, Daddy. I found him myself. I found him up in the horse pasture right after he was born . . . after the stallion was sent away. I know this colt. He's smart. He's beautiful. He's the only foal born on the ranch since we bought it. He belongs here. Sell the mares, but keep him, please keep him."

Daddy was rubbing his chin and staring down at me.

"See, I'm going to start breaking him. The last time we were in town, you know, two weeks ago, I took all my babysitting money and I bought a halter at the Saddlery for him, a halter and a good, soft lead rope. I got the kind that they recommended in a 4-H book. I'm going to start him on lead this vacation and, who knows, come Easter vacation, maybe I can get a saddle on him." I stopped. Daddy was staring at me, his mouth open in disbelief.

"Janey, you don't know a thing about breaking a horse. I admire your sense of adventure, but you'd break your neck before you'd break that colt. He's nothing to play around with. He's got bad blood. Remember his sire—that crazy stallion who kicked out the side of the barn before they got him off the place. His mother throws at least two or three people every year. He's dangerous."

"Oh, Daddy, what do you know about horses?" I stopped. I wanted to bite my tongue. Daddy got that all the time from Grandpa. He was very sensitive about it. It wasn't his fault he wasn't a cowboy like Grandpa. He loved this ranch and he really tried to help with the stock, to ride herd. He just wasn't very good at it.

"What I meant was," I stammered, "what do you or any of us know about this colt? The stallion was crazy because nobody trained him. Grandpa just turned him out in the upper pasture when he was a colt and left him there. Nobody ever tried to break him or get him used to people. He was three years old when we brought him into the corrals. He had his own life out there. Fighting like he did to stay with his mares, well, that was the natural thing. And he was sure smart in the way he did it. Grandpa said so himself. And the mare . . . we got her at auction. How do we know what kind of training she had? Maybe she was mistreated or something. But it's different with the colt. He's been around us. He knows people. He knows *me*. We should have started his training before, but he's only a year and a half. It's not too late. It said so

11

in the book. Oh, please, Daddy, don't sell him. Keep him here."

He shook his head. "Can't, Janey. It just doesn't make sense right now. I've got to cut every possible corner to run this place this year. Try to understand. I'm building this ranch for you kids, for your security. I have to get your college education taken care of, and I have to work fast."

Now *I* was staring out the window. I hated it when Daddy started talking like this to me. I had never thought much about his being older than the other fathers, except when he embarrassed me by wearing funny old clothes. Most of the time he was fun. He took me swimming in the Yellowstone River and ice skating. He read to me and talked to me about important things. He had made the presidential election between Eisenhower and Stevenson really interesting. I could understand what they were talking about because Daddy found things for me to read and helped me. But all this had changed since his heart attack last spring. He told me the doctors said it wasn't serious, but ever since then, he had been talking about getting old and having enough money so we didn't have to worry. It was awful! And every time I argued with him about anything I felt so guilty.

"Janey, I'm going to ask a man named Tom

Yellowfeather to work out here," Daddy continued. "He's Cheyenne. Your grandfather seems to have some nineteenth-century cowboy prejudice, so will you sort of take over and see that the bunkhouse is ready tomorrow? Tom is a good worker. As soon as Henry sees that, I'm sure things will be all right. But try to make everything as smooth as possible in the beginning, will you? Will you do that for me?"

I nodded absentmindedly. I was getting another idea. "Daddy, how about this? This will be good for everyone. Let me buy the colt from Grandpa. Then Grandpa will have money for feed, and when I break the colt there will be another good saddle horse on the ranch."

Daddy laughed. "What would you buy him with?"

"I could cash in those war bonds. You said they belonged to me. I could cash them in and pay Grandpa and. . . ."

"Janey, no! Those bonds are to be used when you really need them. Not for gambling away on an unbroken horse that you may never be able to ride. Don't you understand? You may need those bonds for college."

He wasn't willing to listen to me at all. I started for the door.

"Listen, Janey, your mother's sister and brother will be here soon. She's looking forward to this family gathering, and all the fighting with Grandpa is very hard on her. And you haven't been the easiest person to get along with lately, either. I know it's hard for you, too, right now, but try not to be so moody and impatient. Try to control yourself and help out here this week. Make the holiday a good one—or at least don't ruin it. OK?"

I didn't say anything. Why did I get blamed for being moody and impatient? It wasn't fair.

I glared at him.

"Look, Janey, you can't always get what you want. You can pout and feel sorry for yourself, miss all the fun of Christmas vacation on the ranch, the sledding and skating on the river. But if I were you, I'd count my blessings and enjoy them. Enjoy what you have."

I still didn't answer. It was beginning to snow outside. Big flakes drifted past the window like chicken feathers. Daddy snapped the fasteners on his briefcase and started to the door. He turned around and came back.

"I love you, Janey," he said as he gave me a hug. "I'm only trying to do what is best for you. I'm proud that you are as capable as you are, that you want to do as much as you can out here. You will have your own horse when the timing is better. Just be patient." He hugged me again and left the room.

I sat down on the bed. It was ice cold up here. I hadn't noticed until now. They had let the stove in the hallway burn out. I could see my breath. I pulled the quilt at the end of the bed up around my shoulders. Before long I heard the engine of our pickup truck sputter a time or two, then a roar as it started and the low whine of the tires spinning on the ice. The sound of the engine grew softer as the truck went down the hill; then there was nothing. Nothing. That is how I felt. I had been asking and waiting and trying to be helpful and responsible for a year and a half, ever since the colt was born. Every time I asked when I could have him, Grandpa or Daddy or Grandma or somebody would say, "Just wait a bit, Janey." I waited. I had worked on Grandpa to make sure the colt got branded and gelded so he didn't get wild and start threatening all the other horses as the stallion had done. I hadn't gotten anybody interested enough to help me train him, though. Grandpa said he didn't have time to go messing around teaching him to walk on lead. He said it was stupid to do it that way anyhow. He said the best way was to wait until the colt was about two years old, and then throw a saddle on him and let him buck himself out. Grandpa knew a lot about running cattle and horses, but he didn't know everything. All the books I'd read said it was better to train a horse gradually. I tried to show them to Grandpa, but he laughed at me. He said the day a book could teach him about horses, he'd give up wrangling forever.

Sometimes I hated Grandpa! He was always so right. Anything he wanted or needed was so important, so necessary. But when I wanted or needed something—and not just a toy, either, or a new dress—but something useful, I mean you need a good horse when you work cattle on a ranch, well, forget it. I was spoiled, and I had better learn to make do with what I had. I hated that! They were going to sell the colt, and I knew they'd expect me to keep on riding that old blue plow horse that was way too big for me while I ran cattle for them. They would ask me to do just as much work next summer as I did last year, when I thought I was proving myself. I'd do the work . . . and maybe someday they might think I was worth my own horse, someday when they were good and ready to get it for me. Well, that's what they thought. I wasn't going to put up with it. That colt belonged here. He was born here. He was branded. He was an A6 colt. I'd named him. He was Fire Dancer. Fire, because he was a sorrel, like his father, and in the sunlight his red coat resembled flames. I just liked the name Dancer. I wanted him to have two names, the way the important thoroughbred racehorses did, but I would call him Dancer for short. I would not just sit by while they sold off the colt. I would . . . I didn't know what I'd do. Rolling over on the bed, I pulled the quilt up around my shoulders. I began to cry.

Hollow Holiday

"Janey?" Mom called through the hallway. "Are you still up there? Come on down. I want you to see this."

The dogs were carrying on something fierce. I didn't answer her.

"Janey, I know you're up there. Hurry up. I don't want you to miss it."

I heard the hallway door close. I wasn't going downstairs. I didn't want to see anyone. I got up and went to the window. Grandpa was riding by on Smoky. In the blank, cold light of the snowy day, the big white horse became part of the drifts on the side of the road. Grandpa and the saddle seemed to be floating, and the dark green cedar tree that was dragging behind dangled in white space. The dogs bounded around barking and nipping at the tree as if it was some huge, furry animal. Greg came running out of the house and threw his arms around Pal's neck. Pal jumped to the side and Greg went rolling and laughing in the snow. It was the perfect Christmas scene—"Bringing Home the Tree"—a real old-fashioned picture postcard. But it was all a fake. Christmas was ruined.

"Janey! Why don't you answer me? We're going to decorate the tree. Come on down. We need your artistic eye. Do you hear me?" Mom's voice was edgy. And Daddy said *I* was moody and impatient. There was just no pleasing her anymore.

I knew I could pretend to be asleep, but then she would send Greg up to get me. Finally, I answered, "I'll be down soon." I didn't want to go down. Well, I did sort of, because decorating the tree had always been one of the best parts of getting ready for Christmas. But this Christmas had already lost the very best part.

The dining room stove was roaring and the living room was toasty. The freshly cut tree made the house smell like the cedar gulch does in the warmth of spring when the sap is running.

Grandpa was busy wedging the tree into the small laundry tub. He wasn't talking to anyone. When he got the tree standing right, he left.

Mom and Grandma didn't seem to notice his silence. They were bustling around getting ready to start the decorating. Grandma brought out two big boxes of tinsel rope and glass balls from the closet under the stairs. Each of the glass decorations was wrapped in tissue paper and had to be carefully unwrapped. That was my job. Greg was galloping around with a sprig of cedar Grandpa had trimmed off the tree stuck in the collar of his shirt so that it sprayed out around his head. He was pretending to be a reindeer.

"Watch this, Janey!" He grabbed a piece of tissue paper at the corner and whipped it out from under a red glass ball, the way a magician does a tablecloth from under the dishes on a table. It didn't work. The ball rolled over to the edge and smashed on the floor.

"Greg!" Mom yelled. "That was very stupid. Whatever is the matter with you! Can't you settle down and act decent? Now you can go right. . . ."

"Wait a minute, Lenore," Grandma interrupted her. "He didn't mean to do it. He's excited. I don't think we have ever decorated the tree without breaking one of those things, at least one."

Greg looked as if he were going to cry. He could be a real pain, but I felt sorry for him this time. He was so happy. Christmas is a big time for a little kid. Mom didn't have to carry on like that. I wondered if she knew about the fight. That could be why she was so jumpy. The fights *were* tough on her. She was caught in the middle, since Grandpa and Grandma were her folks. She was a lot younger than Daddy, but sometimes lately her face looked thin and old.

"Look, Greg," Grandma said, holding up a red-and-white glass Santa with a fuzzy cotton beard. "I was saving this one just for you. You find the very best place for him on the Christmas tree."

Grandma was trying to smooth things over. She was good at that. She had to be, I guess, to live with Grandpa all these years. I wished I could count on her to help me keep the colt somehow, but I knew I couldn't. Grandma had never approved of the way I got involved in what she called the "rough stuff" on the ranch: wrangling, branding, calving and the like. Besides, on ranch matters she never crossed Grandpa.

I jerked a small green glass lantern out of its wrapping, and the hook for fastening it to the tree pulled out of the top. Mom saw.

"So, now it's your turn. Please, please watch what you are doing! Honestly, I . . . !"

"Oh, stop it, Mom!" I blurted. This was crazy.

21

So what if Grandpa and Daddy had one of their fights. That was nothing new. This one was a heck of a lot harder on me than it was on her, and I couldn't even talk about it.

"Don't talk to me in that tone of voice, young lady. I just asked you to watch what you are doing. I don't know what gets into you lately." She was looking at me and shaking her head. "You come down here with that long face and act like you have been asked to scrub floors rather than decorate the Christmas tree."

I wanted to throw something, but I jammed my teeth together instead, so I wouldn't be able to answer back and make more trouble.

"Remember this, Janey?" Grandma said, holding up a pretty green bird with red tail feathers. "When you were little you insisted that this be put on the tree where you could touch it. You would give it a tap so it would swing on its branch and then insist that the 'birdie was flying south.' I always thought that was very smart of the birdie, considering the temperatures around here this time of year. Especially since the poor thing looks so tropical."

Grandma's technique worked again. I turned away from Mom to put the bird on the tree. It was a wonderful ornament, and it truly did *seem* to fly through the boughs while bound to a branch. But it wasn't real to me anymore. It was a pretty glass bird with tattered tail feathers.

Greg was rummaging in some boxes on the floor. "What's this?" he asked, holding up a small silver cup. The bottom was indented, and something like a tiny silver clothespin was fastened underneath.

"You'll see," Grandma said, as she took a box of candles, only a little bigger than the birthday-cake kind, out of the same wooden box. She put one of the candles in the silver cup, then clipped the cup, candle and all, to a bough of the Christmas tree. "Come on now. Help me out. Just be careful to keep each candle away from the branches above and beside it. We don't want to *really* light up the tree."

When all the silver cups were scattered about in the outermost branches of the big tree, Grandma brought matches from the kitchen and lit a few of the candles. They burned like small yellow suns. The shiny glass balls became planets orbiting in the cedar universe. It looked as if the pictures in my science book had magically come to life. The candle lights flickered on the frosted windows. Outside, the sky had gone deep purple and gray. The snow floated through it like falling petals from the apple tree. For a moment I felt peaceful, and it was like Christmas.

The back door slammed. There was stomping around in the washroom as Grandpa knocked the snow off his boots and hung up his coat. "Why don't we have any light around here?" he grumbled as he entered the kitchen.

"Come in here, Henry," Grandma called.

He entered the dining room and stared at the tree for a minute.

"We had these lights on the tree out on the homestead. The children were small then. Aren't they beautiful?" Grandma said, more to Grandpa than to us.

"Yeah, they sure beat those colored electric things in town. Now can I get something to eat around here?"

"Of course. What time is it getting to be? It gets dark so early these days. Janey, see that the candles are out. Greg, go close the chicken coop. Take a pan of hot water with you to melt the ice in the water pan. Lenore, you could set the table and have Janey cut fresh bread."

It wasn't long before a pan of hot macaroni and tomatoes was on the table. Grandpa sat down in the chair on the end. In the yellow light of the kerosene lamp, his shadow spread across the cracked, brown paint of the kitchen floor and grew up the wall under the windows. He filled his plate before the rest of us sat down, and he didn't say anything at all.

Grandma's lips were pressed tightly together as she poured his coffee. When she put the pot back on the stove and her back was turned, she asked, "Are you all right, Henry? It was crazy of you to stay out in the cold all day. You should take better care to come in and get warmed up sometimes."

"Nothing wrong with me," Grandpa snapped. "Other people around here are nuts, but I'm just fine."

Mom quickly dropped her eyes to her plate. Grandma came over and sat down at her end of the table. The wood in the cookstove crackled, and some sparks fell down into the ash box.

Grandpa banged his coffee cup down. "Well, Lenore, it seems we'll be getting some help around here. Humph! Some help! Some scab labor off the reservation! That cheap . . . !"

"Henry!" Grandma said sharply.

"Well, it burns me up. Here I told him we could get Jim Gordon back. He's worked the place for two summers. He knows the ranch. I wouldn't have to tell him how to do every little thing, and he'd be here, ready to go come spring. But 'the owner' just up and announces that he's going to hire this Indian. He'll be more trouble than he's worth, most likely, no matter how much he's paid, and I bet he ain't getting much."

"Henry! Stop now. At least we have help coming. You know this winter would have been too much for the two of us—especially for me." Grandma looked at her hands.

I wanted to say something to defend Daddy, but I didn't know what. Grandpa spoke again:

"Well, if this 'help' is just so danged-awful good, we might just leave him here alone for a week or two and take a little trip—go south for your arthritis. We're gonna have a little extra money."

"What are you talking about?" Grandma asked as she got up and began to clear the table.

"It seems that I got my orders to sell off the two mares and that colt. He don't want to feed them through the winter. I'm going to run them into the auction after Christmas. It isn't the best time to sell, but they're good-looking horses and they still have some meat on them from the summer. They'll bring something."

I stared down at the table. Grandma didn't answer him. I could feel her eyes on me. I wasn't going to cry. I would not cry. I wouldn't give any one of them a chance to say "I know how you feel, but. . . ." They didn't know how I felt. They didn't care about the colt. Just about money and getting even with each other. I wished I could go away from them all. Go away to boarding school. I didn't want to live here anymore . . . with their fighting . . . without the colt. I stared hard into the chipped, white glaze of my plate. There, I saw the colt. He was running, running, legs stretched, blond mane flying into my face as I leaned out over his sleek sorrel neck. Purple alfalfa blossoms sent perfume rising up all around us as we galloped through them. I had no bridle, just my hands wrapped in his mane. The picture blurred. My throat began to jump up and down. I would not cry.

"Excuse me," I said, and left the table. I was out the hallway door and into the cold darkness before anyone had a chance to answer me.

"Janey, come back here and help with the dishes," Mom called as I started up the stairs.

"Let her go, Lenore," I heard Grandma say.

Night Venture

There was no lamp in my room. I didn't undress. I wrapped my blankets around me to keep warm and sat in the chair next to my windows. A coyote cried out from the old wheat field by the prairie-dog pasture. After a moment, he was answered from the direction of the cottonwoods down by the river. The snow gathered up in pillow bunches around the sagebrush in front of the ranch house. Falling, slowly falling and drifting. Suddenly, as if it had fallen softly with the snow, the idea came to me. I knew what I must do.

The night seemed to grow brighter. Each snowflake danced down in its own light, like a spark. I watched and waited. Waited for the house to become quiet. When there were no more sounds downstairs, I tiptoed out of my room and down through the kitchen into the washroom. Very quietly, I bundled up and, opening the back door without a squeak, I went out into the wintery night. As I stepped off the back porch, Pal came out from his place beneath it. He came over and rubbed his head against my coat.

"You want to come along?" I asked, patting him. "I'm going all the way down to the horse shed. Can you walk that far in the deep snow?" He reached up and licked my face for an answer. Off we went.

It was so still. We stopped at the horse barn and I went into the tack room. There was only one small window, too small to shed any light at all, but I remembered where I had hung the colt's new halter. I stumbled over a stool and got tangled up in some reins, but I found it. I felt around the floor until my hands grasped the soft lead rope I had left coiled there. Now I was ready. As the barn door swung closed behind me, I looked back at the ranch house. It was all dark. No one had heard me leave. A shiver of excitement wiggled up my spine. I began to run over the path packed by the feed sled, with Pal at my side. When we reached the top of the little hill which dipped into the pasture, I looked down at the bumps and dots, the dark backs of the cattle below me. There was no wind, and they had bedded down in the open rather than take shelter among the cottonwoods or the willows down by the river. I hoped the horses were in the shed, not out there among them. The bulls were down there. They were quite safe, normally, but I didn't know if meandering through their cows in the night would qualify as normal.

Pal tilted his head to one side and waited for me to take the lead. I left the path and headed out along the fence.

It was hard to see the drifts. Every few steps, it seemed, I would sink in up around my knees and have to lean against Pal to pull my legs out. Maybe I should have stayed on the path and chanced the bulls. It was only about a quarter of a mile to the horse shed, but at this rate it was going to take a long time to get there. Pal's dark coat was white with snow now, except where I had knocked it off by leaning on him. The rope halter and the coiled lead which I had draped on my shoulder were stiff with cold. I was glad Pal had come. He waited for me when I had to lift myself out of a drift. He whined at me to hurry up when I was too slow. He was taking care of me as he always had. Daddy gave him to me when I was a baby and he was a pup and we had grown up together.

A coyote howl rose out of the cottonwood trees not far away. I stopped and reached for Pal. Coyotes weren't dangerous to people. I was certain a lone coyote would never come after a person, but the howl was so eerie, rising up like it did out of the bare, twisted winter bodies of the big cottonwoods. Pal whimpered, impatient for us to move on. I knew he wasn't afraid of the coyote. One time he had taken on three of them that were stealing a turkey from Uncle Ed's turkey hutch. Uncle Ed said that he heard the commotion from the shack, went out to see what it was, and there was Pal with a coyote by the scruff of the neck. He was shaking the life out of it while two others cowered beside the hill. Uncle Ed went back into the shack to get his rifle, but by the time he returned, Pal was chasing the coyotes through the cactus and sagebrush at such a pace that Ed couldn't get a shot at them.

The triangular shape of the big lean-to we called the horse shed loomed a few yards in front of me. Now, if only the colt was inside. Old Blue, covered with snow, stood right outside the entrance. He snorted and shook some of the snow off as we passed by him. I peered under the straw overhang of the roof. In the shadows, I could make out Smoky and the black team. Way back in the corner by the mares was the colt. The other horses shifted and backed away slightly as Pal and I entered, but the colt fixed on us with his eyes bright with reflected light from the snow. He whinnied softly and stepped forward, so he stood between us and the mares. In the darkness of the shed, the white-lightning blaze which shot down his face seemed luminous, radiant. He was alive with magnificent power, so like the stallion. I stood quite still before him. I didn't have any idea of how to do this. Pal sat down behind me. I stepped forward, lifting the halter from my shoulder and taking it in my left hand. I reached out to the colt with my right. He snorted and pawed the frozen ground. I stopped.

"Remember me?" I whispered to him.

He turned to face me squarely, his front feet wide, his thick mane falling forward as he lowered his head to sniff my hand through the space between us.

I stepped forward again. "We're going to work together. I'm going to give you your first lesson tonight. We don't have much time to train you. Before I go back to school, that's in just two weeks, I have to be able to lead you. See, I'm going to take you way up in the back pasture. I'm going to hide you there. They won't be able to take you to the auction. You'll have enough hay to keep you through the winter, and come spring, I'll get you and I'll ride you and you will be the best horse in the branding roundup. They'll be glad you stayed."

I moved toward him. He pranced backward, tossing his blond mane and making low purring noises. The mares turned and walked single file to the opposite side of the shed near the team.

The colt reared up on his hind legs, but not high, then spun around to follow them. I stepped forward quickly to block him. I wanted to keep him in the corner, where I had a better chance of getting him to stand still. He stopped short in front of me. I reached out and touched his muzzle. He jerked it up away from me. I'd taken off my mittens. His breath was steamy, hot on my cold, bare hands.

"Whoa! Whoa! Calm down there, boy. You have nothing to be afraid of. I won't hurt you."

He glared at me, his head high.

"Come on, you know me. Remember all the apples and the oats. I've been treating you special ever since you were born. We're friends."

The colt lowered his nose again and snorted. I touched his forehead. Why didn't I bring any oats? That was so dumb of me! He stood as I ran my hands up into the hunk of matted mane between his ears.

"You need to be curried. You've got burrs." He let me scratch between his ears. "You remember me. I know you remember me. See, I knew if I just hung around you, petting you and giving you treats, being good to you, I knew you wouldn't get all crazy-wild like your father. You like me, don't you? Well, now I'm going to put this piece of rope up there by your ears, right where I've been scratching. It will feel like you're getting your head rubbed. That's all." I pulled the top of the halter up with both hands and tried to drape it over his ears. The colt flung his head rapidly to one side. I missed. His mane whipped across my face, stinging my eyes. My hands flew up to protect them, and the halter slid to the ground.

"Now we have to try that again. Just hold still this time." I picked up the halter and held it open with both hands and tried to get the loop around the nose first. The colt shook his head, then stopped and stood quite still as I placed the halter around his nose, then moved it up over his ears. I couldn't believe it! It was too easy. Now all I had to do was fasten the snap hook under his jaw.

"Good boy. Good boy," I repeated excitedly as I held the lead rope and reached under his chin to secure the halter. I had it. Now to fasten it. My fingers were cold and clumsy. The snap lock was strong. It was stiff. I couldn't push it open enough to get the loop into it. The colt pulled back against my hold on the halter. He felt the strange pressure of the rope around his head. He jerked upward. The fastener slipped out of my hands. I grabbed for it again.

"Whoa! Now we've almost got this. You're fine. You're fine," I crooned to him as I struggled with the metal fastener. Suddenly, he sat back on his hind haunches like a donkey, pulling the halter from my grasp. The lead rope was paying through my hand, and the colt turned, swiveled and galloped out the front of the shed. I tried to run after him, but he was too fast. The rope slid through my hands, searing them. He was gone. I stood just outside the shed watching his shadowy form racing deeper into the silvery darkness. Then he stopped. He was standing at the edge of the cottonwoods, watching, waiting, as Pal and I lumbered slowly through the snow toward him. In the half-light, I couldn't see the halter, but the silhouette of the lead rope dangling down into the snow was visible. I had to catch him. I had to get the halter off. That lead rope could tangle in a fence or on a sagebrush and he could get hurt.

My hands and arms were aching with the cold. Sinking into the snow with each step, slowly making my way to where the colt stood, I prayed he would not run again. I was very cold. At least the other horses had stayed in the shed. That was in my favor. Maybe I could herd him back to the mares and could take the halter off there. Suddenly, I realized that I had to take the halter *off*. . . . I had put the halter *on*, first try! The very first time I had tried I got the halter on him. Just the thought boosted me through the snow and up to the colt.

"OK, I'm going to walk right up to you and

take that halter off. It's the end of your first lesson. We've done pretty well. Let's finish it off like professionals. Deal?"

The colt walked away from me into the cottonwood trees, holding his head to one side so he wouldn't step on the lead rope.

"That's smart, but you would be smarter to stand still so I could get it off. Then you wouldn't have to walk that way. Stop right there, now."

He continued to move ahead into the trees. Hurrying after him, I went into a drift up to my thighs. Pal sunk in, too. It took me a while to plow through it to the other side. I was getting tired.

Whooo, whooo, whooo, whooo, whooo.

Five insistent, lingering sounds stopped me in my tracks. I looked up into the trees. It was an owl, I knew it was an owl, but the sound was so haunting. I wanted to see, to be sure. It was scary. I was all alone. No one even knew I was here. I shivered and searched through the lowest cottonwood branches trying to see, but my eyes were bombarded by the constant white dots of falling snow. Pal whined and pushed at my leg. I turned to him and saw that the colt, too, had stopped. He was facing me, alert, listening, watching.

"Good boy. Good boy. Hold it right there."

I was almost up to him when I hit another drift. I tried to go through it slowly, carefully, so

I wouldn't frighten the colt. The snow was heavy. It was like walking upstream in a strong current. Finally, I was within reach of the lead rope. I began, carefully, to gather it into my hands. I moved slowly forward, coiling the rope. I was close to the colt. He did not move. I stood on my toes and tried to lift the halter off. The colt took several prancing steps backward. I waited for him to stop. When he did, he was standing right next to a tree stump. If I could climb up on the stump without spooking him, I could lift the halter off him easily. Holding the lead rope in one hand, slowly, very slowly, I lifted one foot up onto the stump. Keeping that knee bent, I pulled the other foot up behind me. The colt watched me as though he were trying to figure out what in the world I was doing. When I had both feet firmly on the stump, I straightened my knees. I still couldn't get my hands on the halter. The colt was just a little too far away. I tried coaxing him closer by gently pulling on the lead rope. He resisted, pulling back with his head. I let the rope go slack. I waited. In a moment, I pulled again. The rope became taut, then loosened as he took one step forward, then another. Just one or two more and I could reach the halter. I tugged gently again. He moved closer. He was there! I reached out with both hands and grasped the halter behind his ears. I lifted it very very easily, up and over. . . .

CRASH . . . *Yip, Yip* . . . *Crack*! Branches breaking, howling in the willows down by the river. The colt whinnied. His body flew up above me, his hooves striking at the air, then he blended into the blackness before my eyes. My knees crumpled and I was falling.

Grrrrrrrrrrrr! Pal's head was above me. His teeth were bared, lips curled back. His throat vibrated with the strength of his growl. I tried to lift myself out of the snow. There was a dark spot in the snow beneath my face. My mouth hurt. My chin throbbed. I tasted something salty, blood. *Grrrrrrr*. Pal's growling didn't stop. I tried to see into the darkness. Why was he growling? A few feet in front of me was the shadowy shape of the halter lying in the snow. I reached for it. Pal's growl grew louder, more menacing. Just as my fingers closed about the rope, I saw something move among the trees. A whining arose from the shadows and drifts, until it became a howl and shot through the air. Two sets of yellow eyes floated before me, then two more. They disappeared behind a tree. Then a tearing sound. . . . A picture flashed before me of the old canvas tent splitting in two when the tree branch caught on it during a windstorm. Snarling, panting . . . more growling, and not from Pal. Eyes, yellow, golden, rising up from behind a drift. I reached up until my hands found Pal's fur and gripped. I pulled. I had to get up, to move. A pair of eyes moved toward us. Pal stiffened. The hair on his back rose and his growl roared forth. I struggled to stand. *Grrr!* Pal lunged forward at the coyote just as it sprang at us. The coyote leaped up into the air and turned at the same time. He seemed to vaporize, disappear into a blur of snowflakes.

"Run, run, run, run, run," beat like my pulse through me. Holding on to Pal, I turned and tried to move. I tripped and fell over a dead branch. Pal stayed with me until I was standing again. I wrapped the halter around my arm, the lead rope dangled behind. As we tried to run through the snow, it caught on a sagebrush and jerked me back. I untangled it and we hurried on, out of the cottonwoods, through the pasture, this time cutting through the cows, not worrying about the bulls. I fell down again. As my face hit the snow, the cold sent pain like an icicle razor blade through my lower lip and jaw.

At last we reached the back porch. It wasn't until we were in the washroom that I began to cry. I put my head on the thick, coarse hair of Pal's neck to muffle my sobs and cried and cried . . . from fear—and from relief. I was so frightened. My mouth hurt, but it seemed that the bleeding had stopped. I didn't even know for sure what had happened. The halter . . . I was taking off the halter, then there were noises and the colt reared. Maybe he bumped me with his head as he reared, and knocked me off the stump, knocked me out. Oh . . . then the coyote . . . shivers shot through me. I was still scared, but I couldn't tell anyone. I didn't want to go upstairs alone. I didn't want to leave Pal. He had taken care of me . . . maybe saved me. As though he knew I was thinking about him, he turned his head and licked my face.

"Come on, boy," I said. He followed me silently, questioningly, through the still-warm kitchen, through the hallway and up to my room. He knew he wasn't allowed to sleep in the house. I sat down on my bed. Pal put his head in my lap and gently licked my hand as though he were telling me that everything was all right now. I hugged him, then pulled my quilt up over me and lay down without even getting undressed.

Defiance

"**J**aney, get up now."

It seemed as though the call was floating in thick darkness. I tried to answer, but there was something between me and my own voice. My mouth, my jaws were fastened shut and hurting. Slowly, I opened my eyes. I was in my bed with my coat, scarf, and boots on. Pal was lying on the rug beside the bed. There were dark stains on the quilt, which was pulled up around my face.

"Janey! Do I have to come up and drag you out of bed? Come on! Grandpa needs you," Mom shouted up the stairs.

I pushed myself up and sat on the edge of the bed. My scarf was stiff and stuck to my face. The halter, which had been so clean and white yesterday, now lay in a heap on my bedroom floor with brown blotches, like tobacco spit, all over it. Pal sat up and put his head on my knees. He looked up at me and I saw again those eyes, those other eyes, glowing in the snow. Huge bird's wings of fear beat against my chest as I remembered what had happened.

"Answer me, Janey! Will you *please* answer me before I have to come up there. You are not the Queen of Sheba. You cannot sleep until noon. Breakfast is ready and there is work to be done."

"Yes, yes, yes! I'll be down in a few minutes," I croaked back at her.

I stood up and walked over to my dresser. I looked into the mirror. Horrible! My lower lip was swollen and purple. There were smeared blobs of dark brown all around my face . . . dried blood. My hair was matted with crusty brown near my ear. Red fuzz from my wool scarf stuck in the dark spot on the corner of my mouth.

I spit on my fingers and tried rubbing at the blood stains. They smeared. I took a bandana from my drawer and spit on it, then tried wiping my face. Where did all the blood come from? There was a split inside my mouth under my lower lip. I must have bitten it when the colt's head hit mine or when he knocked me off that tree stump. I was knocked out! I didn't even know how long . . . a minute, ten minutes. Suddenly, my hands flew to my eyes as if they could block the image of the coyotes . . . the coyotes, the snarling, the tearing sound. Maybe that didn't happen. Maybe I dreamed it when I was knocked out.

"Janey! I'm not going to call you again!"

"Coming."

I took off my coat and my boots and started for the kitchen carrying them. I didn't know what I would tell them about my face, about Pal who was coming along behind me. Partway down the stairs, I remembered I'd left the halter lying in the middle of the floor. What if Mom or someone went into my room and found it? I ran back up and shoved it under my bed. When I finally opened the kitchen door I ran smack into Mom, who was coming up to get me.

"It's about time, young lady!" she began, then stopped and stepped back from me and stared. "Janey! What happened to you?"

Grandma turned from the stove and Grandpa looked up from his plate. Pal stepped up beside me and rubbed against my leg.

"Well . . . ?" Mom stood, both hands on her hips, waiting for an explanation.

I looked down at Pal. I knew I was going to tell a lie. I didn't know what it would be. I scratched my head and waited for it to come.

"What is it, Janey? What happened to you?" Grandma asked. Her voice sounded soft and sympathetic.

I began: "I woke up in the middle of the night and had to go to the outhouse. When I was coming back up the hill . . . a . . . a rabbit or something came running, and Pal, he was with me, started barking, and I got scared and tried to hurry and slipped on some ice and fell down and cut my lip. I was too tired to take care of it, and, besides, it wasn't too bad, so I just went to bed. . . ." I waited for their response.

"Poor thing," Grandma said "I wish you had gotten me up to help you. I was very tired last night. Must have slept very soundly. I didn't hear a thing . . . no barking, nothing. Well, let me take a look at that lip and get your face sponged off, then you can have some pancakes. Maybe she shouldn't ride today, Henry."

"Don't see why not," Grandpa said as he stared hard at me. "Never knew a cut lip interfered with riding." He picked up his cigarette and took a long draw. When he blew the smoke out it curled slowly through the air in front of his face. He continued to look at me through the gray-white spirals.

"It's nothing," I said quickly to Grandma. "I'm OK. I can ride."

Grandma came over and took my chin in her

44

hand. She lifted my face and carefully touched my lower lip. Her hands were warm from working over the stove. They felt so good. I wanted to be little again, to sit on her lap and cry and tell her what really happened.

"A good-size cut inside your mouth . . . looks like you chomped down on it with your upper teeth. Not much we can do for an injury inside the mouth. Can't put antiseptic on it . . . just make sure you keep your language clean!" She wrinkled her forehead and looked stern, then laughed. "Sit down and start your pancakes." Grandma turned to the stove.

Mom was silently sipping her coffee as I sat down at the table.

"Where's Greg?" I asked her, just to make conversation.

"He's up in his room reading comics, I guess. He ate early. We're baking cookies today. I promised I'd call him when it's time to roll and cut them."

Grandma came back with a warm, wet washcloth. She sponged off my face, gently dabbing around my lower lip. "There, that's much better. Now hurry up with your breakfast so you can go to the barn with Grandpa."

Grandpa was staring at me over the rim of his coffee cup. His eyes seemed to be pressing on me. I could hardly breathe. Finally he said:

"Funny thing . . . there weren't any tracks through the new snow going to the outhouse this morning. There were some down by the horse shed, though." He paused and slowly, deliberately snuffed out his cigarette on his plate. I was afraid to even chew. Suddenly, he slammed his cup down on the table and leaned forward: "Now I don't know for certain what you're up to, but I got a good idea. I'm telling you this, and I'm telling you just once! Stay away from that colt! He's range rank and clean. He's strong and he can send you flying through the air and tromp you so's you'd look like a pile of dirty clothes. If you go messing with that colt again, I'll toss you around the north forty. You don't know nothing about this horse. Any unbroken horse for that matter. You'd wind up either kicked or trampled, or the horse would get tricky and kid-spoiled. That colt is his father's son, smart and mean. So just stay away from him!"

There was silence. I tried to cut my pancakes. My fork slipped and clanged loudly against my plate. Grandma brought the blue enamel pot over and poured Grandpa some coffee. When she turned to go she bumped against Pal's foot, and he stood up to get out of her way.

"That dog isn't supposed to be in here. Put him out!" Grandpa ordered.

Mom was looking down into her plate and I

saw her nod toward the door, meaning I should do as he said. I felt something hard and hot, a flaming coal, burning in my chest. Grandpa was furious with me. I knew how he could be when he was mad. One time Smoky didn't cut as close in on a stray steer as Grandpa wanted. Grandpa pulled the horse up short, hopped down off his back and grabbed a big hunk of cottonwood stick that was lying on the riverbank. He slammed Smoky in the flanks with it. Every time Smoky jumped to get away from the blows, Grandpa jerked so hard on the reins that the bridle bit cut into the horse's mouth. Now it seemed as though he wanted to do something like that to me. Well, he just couldn't treat me that way!

"Take him out," Grandpa repeated, his voice low and raspy.

"He's tired, and he isn't bothering anyone," I answered so calmly it surprised me.

Mom left the table and pretended to be busy with something at the stove. Grandma had gone into the pantry.

"Janey, do as I say . . . *now!*"

"No!" After the word came out, I felt dizzy.

"Then I'll take him out!" Grandpa said quietly, but with a fury that seemed to fill the whole room like a whirling wind. He rose and took a step toward me.

"Henry!" Grandma shouted as she hurried

back into the kitchen. "Janey!" She turned to me with a pleading look. "Put the dog in the washroom. He'll be fine there. It's warmer than it is under the porch."

I knew I had do something . . . but not exactly what they said. I had some rights. If I couldn't have a horse, at least I could have my dog. "I'll take him out with me when I go," I said as firmly as I was able.

"Then leave. Get on up to the barn now!" Grandpa ordered.

I looked up at him. He was still holding his coffee cup. I looked right at him as I said, "I have to work this morning and I'm hungry. I'll go when I've finished my breakfast." Why was I doing this? I was terrified.

"Listen, kid. I'm not taking another word out of that sassing mouth of yours." He put his coffee cup down on the table and started for me. Grandma stepped in between us.

"OK!" I heard myself shouting. "OK! Sure! You can make me take my dog out of the kitchen this very minute! I do the work of a hired hand and you treat me like a child who isn't entitled to have her own dog in the house when he is old and sick and it's freezing cold outside. But I can see what you're doing. I can see how you are. You have to be right all the time, boss all the time—even if you're wrong."

48

"Janey!" Grandma cut in. "Get up to the barn! The blue horse is saddled. Go down and run the strays out of the river pasture and into the feeding pasture."

I got up from the table. Pal followed me into the washroom. I stopped there to put on my coat and things. I was more angry than frightened now. What could they do to me? So what if Grandpa hit me . . . so what! I couldn't be hurt any more than I had been already by losing the colt.

Old Blue was saddled and tied to the corral waiting for me. I climbed on and headed for the river pasture. The clouds and the snow came together on the edge of the field below the barn hill in a cold, thin line. The prairie dog mounds were bumps under the flat, white snow sheet. Blue ambled along. I felt tired and kind of woozy. It was hard to concentrate on the work. Lucky for me, Blue was quick and kept a couple of steers from cutting back into the woods when we had them at the gate. It didn't take us too long to get all twenty-three head moving into the feeding pasture.

Grandma and Grandpa had stopped the feed sled next to the haystack and were filling the big sled box when I shut the gate. I dreaded it, but I knew I had to ride over and report how many cattle I'd found to Grandpa.

I covered the distance quickly. When he saw me coming, Grandpa stopped forking hay and leaned on the sled box and waited. I told him how many strays I'd found.

"Good. That accounts for all of them," Grandpa said, and without the slightest nod of thanks he returned to Grandma and said, "Sled's full and this load should do it. Let's go, Marie."

She sat down on the springboard seat and unwrapped the reins from the sled brake. In a moment they were winding in and out among the cattle, Grandpa forking hay off the back of the sled and Grandma negotiating the course between the cattle, the salt blocks and the sagebrush. It was fiercely tough work, physically hard on the one who pitched hay and on the driver, too, who had to spend hours at a time in freezing cold. Watching them, I realized they were too old for such hard work. They *did* need help. Well, they were going to get it. And Daddy was going to have hay for his cattle, too. They were going to sell the colt so everyone could get what he needed. Everyone except me. I didn't count. I was just a dumb kid.

I turned Blue and headed into the cottonwoods, deep into them, along the edge of the river. The willows stuck up out of the drifts like stiff, crooked broomsticks. I rode through them and out onto the snow-covered ice of the river. I let Blue take a drink at the water hole. I knew

Grandpa had chopped it out earlier this morning, but a thin layer of ice was forming on the edge already. It must be colder than it seemed. I rode around the pasture, staying in the trees, out of sight, until I was sure Grandma and Grandpa had gone back to the barn. Then I pointed Blue toward the horse shed. He thought we were heading for home, so he was willing to gallop where the snow wasn't deep. We got there in no time. I spotted the colt standing alone. He had seen us coming and his head was high, nose up in the wind as though he was catching our scent. How proud, how beautiful he looked. His dark red coat was like the red shale hills at sunset. As I drew near, he perked up his ears. His eyes were bright and curious. His coat had grown thick and shaggy for winter. I could hardly see the A6 which had been burned into his hide last summer.

Dancer moved in closer. I could see the yellow flecks around the dark centers of his eyes. Slowly, I lifted my mittened hand from the saddle horn and reached into the space between us. Dancer stopped. I stopped. My hand was suspended in the wintery air. Neither of us moved. I wanted to touch him so badly. He was very near.

"Come on. Just a little closer. Just a little," I pleaded in a whisper.

He swung his head to the side and shook his

mane. He was thinking about it. He took a step closer. I could almost reach him. He took another step. The tips of my mittened fingers were just a hair away from the white streak on his forehead.

"One more. One more," I whispered, then held my breath as Dancer lowered his head, preparing to take another step. I wished I'd brought the halter so I could make another try. What was I thinking? How could I still be thinking that after Grandpa's threats? I was . . . I looked at the colt and I knew I would try again.

Suddenly, Blue shied. He jerked to the side so abruptly I had to grab for the saddle horn to keep from being tossed. Then he stopped dead and backed up, shaking his head and snorting.

"Whoa! Whoa!" I patted his neck to calm him. Then I saw it. Lying half-buried in the new snow but still red with freshly frozen blood was the gnawed carcass of a doe. The belly was ripped and the bared bones of the front leg stuck up out of a drift, the pointed black hoof striking at the air.

A long, high-pitched whinny sliced through the cold. Just as I looked up, the colt spun on his back legs, rearing and turning, then gathered his body like a spring and leaped forward, galloping wildly out across the pasture. Blue shook nervously and tried to get hold of the bit so he could follow. My knees began to tremble, shiver. Again I saw the eyes, heard the tearing, the ripping of flesh. My teeth chattered. There really had been coyotes here last night feeding off this doe. The sounds, the crashing sounds I had heard before the colt jumped, before everything went black, must have been the doe struggling in the frozen underbrush. I gave Blue a kick, and we lurched ahead together, hurrying away, hurrying home.

When I got to the barn, I put Blue in a stall and left him for Grandpa to unsaddle. I couldn't wait to get home. I ran down from the barn and was out of my wraps and in the warm kitchen in a few minutes. Grandma was putting together something for lunch and Mom and Greg were cleaning up the cookie dough from the table.

"We're going to have a bite to eat as soon as your grandfather gets here. Come and warm up by the stove until then," Grandma said to me as though nothing had happened, as though everything was just the same as it always was, as though there had been no fight with Grandpa.

I was relieved at first, then I got angry. For them it *was* just the same. . . . *I* was the same, the same little kid doing whatever they told me to do. Well, I wasn't!

"I don't feel like eating lunch," I said, and went right through the kitchen, into the hallway, and up the stairs. I was surprised when no one called after me or tried to stop me. I threw a couple good-sized sticks of wood in the potbelly. Let them lecture me about saving wood. I'll sure tell them. I certainly had the right to a few sticks of wood for all the work I did around here.

The door to my room had been closed all morning, so what heat there was hadn't gotten into it. It was like an icebox. After I checked under my bed to see that the halter was still there, I lay down. My quilt was bloodstained—a mess. Everything was a mess. I wished I could cry. I pulled the quilt up over me and tried to go to sleep, but my mouth hurt and my jaw ached. How had everything gotten so rotten all of a sudden?

Friday night, just three days ago, I was in the Christmas play at school. I played my part very well. Mom and Daddy had been so proud. I was happy with the presents I had to give to the family. I made most of them. I knitted Grandpa a thick wool muffler, a red one. I made it to keep him warm, because he was out in the cold so much, and because it would go well with the red-and-black checkered flannel shirts he always wore. He probably wouldn't wear it now because it came from me. I went over to my suitcase and took out my Grimm's fairy tale book. I'd been reading this book for years. I could close my eyes and see the illustrations for each story from memory, but I never got tired of it. I kept it in my suitcase because I didn't want Mom and Grandma to know I still read it, that I carried it with me back and forth between the ranch and the depot.

"Janey, supper," Grandma was calling softly into my darkened room.

I lifted my book off my face and told her I would be right down. She told me to hurry and went back downstairs, leaving me alone. I didn't know how long I had been sleeping. Through my window, I could see the Big Dipper hanging over the bluff across the river with the North Star shining bright as an electric porch light. I got up and went into the hallway. The smells of supper came drifting upstairs. I was starving! Because of my sore mouth and my fight with Grandpa I hadn't been able to eat much breakfast, then I skipped lunch. Grandpa! I dreaded seeing him. Reporting to him out in the pasture was one thing, sitting across the table from him was another. Suddenly, supper didn't seem so important. I would tell Grandma and Mom that I didn't feel well and come back upstairs. After everyone went to bed, I'd sneak down for some leftovers.

"Janey, come in here," Grandma called from the kitchen.

I opened the door, but stood in the hallway. "I don't feel very well. I'm going to skip dinner."

Grandma turned away from the stove and

looked at me. Mom and Greg were playing cards at the table and didn't pay attention. Grandma held my eyes with hers for a long time.

"Come in here for a moment," she said, as she moved toward the dining room door.

I followed her. It was dark and cold. There had been no fire in the dining room stove since we had decorated the tree. It smelled like Christmas, though, and in the lamplight, which filtered through the crack Grandma left in the door, the tinsel and glass balls shimmered.

"Janey, I want you to apologize to your grandfather," Grandma said right off.

I didn't answer.

"You talked to him in a way that I've never heard anyone talk to him . . . and get away with it. You know why? Because he thinks the world of you. He's taken you with him into situations I wished he hadn't; but he took you because you wanted to go, and because he wanted you to have the chance to learn as much about the ranch as you could. It wasn't always easy for him, but he never told you when you were a burden. When he took you on those long trail rides when you were just a little tyke, did you know that he was always circling back to see if you were OK? No, you only knew that he scolded you when you made a mistake. He didn't *want* you to think that you had to be taken care of. He wanted you to

56

feel that you were capable. He never sold you short, Janey. Now, I've been watching you . . . and you've been selling Grandpa short for some time—ever since he tied that log chain to the stallion, I think. Janey, he's not always right, I know that. But give him credit where credit's due."

Grandma stopped, put her fingers over her lips and sighed. She waited for my answer. I was thinking about what she had said, but I wasn't sure that she was right about him.

"What about how he talked about Daddy, Sunday night? What about the way he *always* has to be right—thinks he's the only one who knows about things, like the colt, like the stallion. He says they're mean. He never even tried to work with either of them. He just decides they're mean. And what about the help, Mr. Yellowfeather. Grandpa says he won't be any good because he is an Indian. He fights with Daddy and makes all kinds of trouble over it when he doesn't even know. He just has a dumb idea!"

"I'm not denying that your grandfather is a stubborn, bullheaded old man, but it's hard for him to work for your father, to take orders from someone who has no experience ranching. Remember your grandfather has been ranching since he was fifteen. Not much older than you are now. He ran away from home then, ran away

57

from his education. This life is all he knows, but he does know it. He knows ranching and cattle and horses very well. Your father doesn't quite understand the practical end of it. He makes mistakes, and Grandpa has to take care of righting them; yet he doesn't have any authority here. Right now, Grandpa is worried sick over the way the winter is building up. We've had too much snow and cold for this time of year. We had to start feeding the cattle earlier than usual. If the weather gets worse in January and February, we're going to run out of hay . . . because your father bought those extra cows in September. Now your father is most concerned about the bookkeeping, the money. Well, nothing is going to balance out if a blizzard comes and we run out of feed. We could lose half the herd." Grandma hissed the last words with such force that I stepped back from her. "As for Grandpa and the Indian help. . . . It's true that he would rather have Jim Gordon work here, because he knows the place and works well with Grandpa. But I'll tell you something . . . if this man your father has hired does the work well, your grandfather will treat him fairly, which is more than I can say for someone who hires an Indian because he can get away with paying less."

Grandma had pulled herself up straighter and straighter as she spoke. Now she stood taller than me, even though we were the same height. I wanted to say something to defend Daddy. I knew she was wrong to think that he would pay Tom Yellowfeather less money. Daddy was very fair. Before I could say anything, she went on:

"This is an important holiday, Janey. Our family will be together for the first time in years. God knows if there will be another chance. It is no time to fight. Please apologize to your grandfather. Try to understand his position, his pressures." Grandma was pleading with me now. "Janey, I'll tell you a secret. I don't have arthritis. I just pretended so Grandpa would ask for the extra hand. Grandpa's the one who isn't well. He's had some pains lately, but he wouldn't ask for help for himself. He's too proud to let anybody think he's getting on, that he can't do the job. Janey, don't judge him so harshly. Don't be as righteous and one-sided as you claim he is. No matter what you think, Grandpa cares about the stock, about this ranch, and a great deal about you. He's putting the last good years of his life into this place, and he's probably going to die here with all the cattle and the horses that don't even belong to him." Grandma stepped forward and put her hands on my shoulders. For a moment, I though she was going to shake me the way Mom did sometimes. Instead, she looked directly into my eyes. Hers were glistening behind her glasses. "He loves you, Janey. Try to understand him."

"Where's Marie?" Grandpa asked Mom in the kitchen. I hadn't heard him come into the house.

There was the clomp, clomp of his boots crossing the kitchen floor. A shadow fell through the light in the crack in the door.

"Marie," he called into the darkness.

"I'll be right there," Grandma answered, still gripping my shoulders. "Will you apologize?" she whispered.

"Marie, what's going on in there?"

I nodded *yes*. She hurriedly kissed me on the cheek and went to meet Grandpa at the door. I would do it for Grandma. I would try to make peace. Some of the things she had said made me think, too. Maybe she was right. I never knew that Grandpa had to take care of me, that I was work when I rode with him. I always thought I was helping him, and that he was really cranky when he bawled me out. But I could see now that maybe he was teaching me . . . doing his job and teaching me, too. Everything was complicated. . . .

I stayed alone in the fragrant darkness of the dining room for a few minutes trying to get up the nerve to go in and face Grandpa. When I did, everyone was already seated at the table for supper. I took my place. The kerosene lamp flared and began to smoke up the chimney. Grandma got up and trimmed the wick. Silverware clinked against the plates.

Grandma stared at me over her coffee cup. She nodded slightly. I knew I was supposed to speak. I couldn't. I started, "Gra . . ." then stopped. Grandpa looked up from his plate. I tried again.

"Grandpa . . . I've been thinking . . . about the way I acted at breakfast." I hurried on now, wanting to get it over with. "I know I was cranky and said some pretty disrespectful things. I . . . I'm sorry. I guess I was. . . ." I didn't know what I wanted to say I was. "Well, I'm just sorry, that's all."

Grandpa was poking at his teeth with the tine of his fork. He didn't answer me, but he nodded slightly, then buttered a slice of bread.

Grandma smiled at me from across the table.

Then, as if an invisible "Silence" sign had disappeared from the room, the kitchen came to life.

"Tomorrow we bake the pies," Grandma planned out loud.

"You'll have the whole day for it, too," Grandpa said. "If the new help comes, he'll do the feeding for you." He looked over at Greg. "And I've got a job for you in the morning."

Greg looked at Grandpa, his eyes big with sur-

61

prise. Grandpa hardly ever paid any attention to him. Greg didn't like to do many ranch things. He was afraid of the horses sometimes, and Grandpa usually had no patience with him.

"Yep, someone has to go out and pick up the mail tomorrow. I guess it's about time you gave it a try. I'll saddle up Old Blue for you. You can see if you can get him to go through those drifts—play pony express," Grandpa said to Greg.

I couldn't believe it. Getting the mail had been my job for years . . . and I always rode Blue.

"What do you say? You want to try?" Grandpa asked Greg.

Whether he wanted to or not, Greg was happy to be noticed by Grandpa. I knew the feeling. "Sure!" Greg answered, grinning from ear to ear.

I stared down into my plate. I saw what Grandpa was doing. Lot of good it did me to apologize. He wasn't going to let me get away with only an apology. He was going to show me I couldn't act like that with him . . . teach me my place! He was taking away Blue, the only horse on the ranch I had to ride. He was taking away my job. Well, I had to give Grandpa credit for one thing . . . not sell him short on this. When he wanted to break you down, he knew how to do it. Horses, people . . . he knew how to hurt. I blinked back my tears. Grandpa shoved his chair away from the table and went over to the stove to get a match to light his cigarette.

"May I please be excused?" I asked.

"Of course," Grandma answered, looking at me strangely. She knew what Grandpa was doing, too.

"May I take a lamp upstairs?" I asked over-politely after I had cleared the table.

"Take the one out of my room," Mom said. "I'm not going to read tonight."

"Thank you and good night," I said, trying to sound adult and businesslike.

Upstairs, I sat down on my bed in the dark. I didn't go get the lamp. Why, why did Grandpa have to do that! Just to show me that he was the big boss? To make me get down on my hands and knees and tell him I was sorry I had talked back to him? To get me to beg him not to take Blue away from me, too? Well, I wouldn't!

Through the silvery frost on the windows, I could see the shadow of a cloud on the snow as it covered the moon. Then:

Whooo, whooo, whooo, whooo, whooo.

Like five wind sounds, low and distant. I wasn't frightened by the call, not here in my room, but it reminded me of last night, of the colt. How he stopped and listened, too. Had he, too, felt the mystery of the sound . . . or was he sensing the danger of the coyotes that had been so near. I wondered if he was listening now.

Storm

The wind was howling through the cracks in the shingles, sending biting breezes like tiny stinging bullets into my room. My closet door banged against the wall as a gust of wind blasted up under the eaves. It banged again. I jumped out of bed to close it. The floor was freezer-locker cold, even through my socks. I hopped across the floor trying not to stay too long at a time in one spot. When the closet door was secured with the hook, I tiptoed quickly to the rug by the window. I couldn't see anything but white. The white of the frosted pane seemed to have thickened and spread right out off the roof of the porch. I pressed my elbow, wrapped in my flannel shirt and long underwear, against it and rubbed a clear spot. It didn't help much.

Brrrrrrrr. It was very cold. The stove must have gone out in the night, or I had slept very late. I couldn't tell the time by the light. It could be nine or noon. I decided to go downstairs and check. One thing was certain, I thought, smiling as I pulled on my jeans. Grandpa wasn't going to send Greg out on Blue to the mailbox in this weather. I looked into the mirror. My lip wasn't as swollen as it had been yesterday, the bruise on my face was more green than purple. I ran a brush through my hair, not bothering to redo my braids, and headed for the kitchen.

"Well, you're up early," Grandma commented as I burst into the room. "What do you think of this weather? Rotten, isn't it?"

"I love it," I said defiantly.

Grandma had been putting some wood into the stove. She turned and looked at me, wrinkling her forehead. "Well, I don't! If this keeps up, the whole place will look like the good Lord wrapped it up in freezer paper and put it in the locker marked 'Not To Be Thawed Until Easter.' "

I had to smile, thinking about the prairie as the good Lord's piece of beefsteak to be thawed for his Easter dinner. "Well, do you think he might thaw it out a few days early for the Last Supper?" I asked Grandma.

"Don't you get smart, young lady!" she snapped, but I could see she was holding back a smile.

I looked around the kitchen. "Where is everybody?"

"Your mother and Greg took some boiling water up to the chicken coop to deice the water pans again. We have to keep those old hens happy enough to bring us a few eggs a day. Grandpa went up to the barn. He kept the team in the barn overnight. Said he thought it was going to storm."

If Grandpa knew it was going to storm, I wondered why he made such a big deal of asking Greg to go to the mailbox.

"Janey, thank you for apologizing to him. It helped. I know he wasn't too gracious, but remember he's a proud man."

I wished that Grandma could see my side as clearly as she seemed to see Grandpa's. She would understand about me and the colt. I remembered two years ago when there had been a bad storm. Grandma and Grandpa ran out of supplies. Grandpa couldn't leave because he had to feed the cattle, so Grandma walked out to the county road hoping to get a ride to town with the mailman. But the county road was blocked and the mailman couldn't get through. Rather than turn back, Grandma walked ten miles to the paved highway and caught a ride to town. She got supplies, and got a ride back the next day with the man who came to plow out the county road. It was very brave of Grandma to go out alone in that weather. If a storm had come up when she was walking to the highway, she might have lost her way and frozen to death. I asked her why she decided to go on when the mailman didn't come. Why she took that big risk rather than wait for another day. They wouldn't have starved. I remembered her answer: "I didn't care if it seemed crazy for an old lady to go tromping off through the drifts by herself. As far as I was concerned, I had the best reason in the world for doing it. I wanted to see if I could." Everyone thought that was a terrific answer, a great attitude. Why didn't they understand that I felt the same way about the colt? I only wanted a chance to try.

"Janey, where have you gone off to? I said thank you," Grandma said, looking at me as though I should say "you're welcome."

I didn't say anything. The dogs began barking. Grandma and I both went to the window. Through the thick frost on the pane, we could see a car cresting the hill. It was a moment before we could hear the sound of the engine over the wind. Grandma looked at me, raised her eyebrows, and shrugged. The ranch house was more than two miles off the main road. Even though it was on the flats, where the wind kept the road from drifting shut, traveling wasn't easy in the winter. We didn't get much drop-in company.

The car, an old black Ford, pulled up beside the porch. A tall man in a plaid jacket and a beat-up cowboy hat got out.

"I'll bet it's the new help," Grandma said as she headed for the door.

The Yellowfeathers! Daddy had asked me to check the bunkhouse. I had forgotten completely. I'd have to go up there right now and see what they needed to get settled . . . and once I was out of the house I could sneak down to the horse shed and take a look at the colt. Surely, when it was storming like this, the horses would be in the shed. I wouldn't try to bring the halter, because it would be hard to take him out of the shed, but I could pet him. Keep him used to me. Later, maybe when it stopped snowing, I'd go down with the halter. I was going to stick to my plan despite Grandpa's threats. I went into the washroom.

"Here's my granddaughter. She can show you up to the bunkhouse. As soon as you get settled in, I know my husband could use a hand with the feeding. He hasn't gone out yet, he was hoping it might clear," Grandma went on as I put on my boots and things. "If you need anything, just tell Janey."

Mr. Yellowfeather nodded to me as he opened the door, and we went out on the porch together. "The bunkhouse is up here. Just follow me," I said to him as he got into his car. Inside, I saw a large woman with a scarf around her head sitting in the front. A boy's face looked over the back of the seat, shiny dark hair lying on his forehead like a blackbird's wing.

I ran across the yard ahead of the car to the bunkhouse. As I stepped inside, the floor groaned and creaked with the cold. I went over to the cupboard and checked to see that there were two kerosene lamps. The place was in fair shape. There were two small rooms, each with windows covered in flowered print curtains made from chicken-feed sacks. One room held the cookstove, a table, and four chairs. There were some cupboards on the wall in the corner with a washstand beneath them. In the other room were four metal beds. They stood bare; the mattresses were piled in the corner with some brownish-green army blankets folded and stacked on top of them. It wasn't dirty, but it wasn't cozy either. I should have at least come up and gotten wood and water before they arrived.

The car pulled up at the stoop. I hurried outside to help them. Mr. Yellowfeather went around to the trunk and opened it. He spoke in Cheyenne, and his wife answered him as she got out of the car. The boy went immediately to the back of the car. While I stood there, wondering what to do, they carried on a conversation with each other in Cheyenne at the back of the car. Finally, the boy came around carrying a box of groceries. His mother called something to him and he laughed as he climbed the stairs. I knew him. His name was John. He'd gone to my school. I started to say hello, but he walked quickly past me. His mother followed him with another box. This one was full of clothes.

"I will go get you some water," I said very slowly to Mrs. Yellowfeather as she went by. I didn't know if she spoke English, but I went ahead: "You will need some wood, too. The woodpile is right behind the bunkhouse. I will get you some now, then later I can show you where it is."

Mrs. Yellowfeather was taking groceries out of the box and spreading them on the table. She spoke again in Cheyenne. John came out of the bedroom.

"My mother says to show me now where the well and the woodpile are. I can bring what we need." He spoke with an accent. Each word was neatly clipped away from the one before it and after it.

"Fine," I said and picked up the enamel bucket sitting on the washstand. "The well is down by the house."

He nodded toward the door. I went out and he followed me, past the car where his father was sorting through a toolbox and down to the well in front of the ranch house. He pumped the bucket full. We walked back to the bunkhouse. Neither of us spoke. I didn't know what to say. Maybe he didn't recognize me. He hadn't been at school for over a year. I showed him where the woodpile was and helped him by carrying an armload of split wood to the bunkhouse. His mother had started a small fire in the cookstove with some cardboard and some kindling left in the woodbox since last summer. I didn't know what else I should do for them. The place was beginning to heat up. It didn't take long with such low ceilings. Mrs. Yellowfeather picked up the box of clothes and took them into the bedroom. She had taken off her head scarf, and one long, dark braid fell over the shoulder of her sweater. John was standing by the stove rubbing his hands together over the top.

"I'll be going now. If you need anything more, just come down and knock at the door. My dog might bark at you. . . ." I stopped. What a dumb thing to say. I was babbling. I only wanted to get away and get some time with the colt before Mr. Yellowfeather was done here and went to feed cattle with Grandpa. I had to get there before they did. It would spoil everything, if Grandpa saw me.

"I hope everything is OK. I'll check on you later," I said abruptly, and stepped out the door. John waved to me, but he didn't show that he knew me at all. I wondered how old he was. He had been a grade behind me in school, but he seemed older now.

As I left the bunkhouse, Pal came running. He wiggled all over, he was so glad to see me. Together, we waded through the big drift by the fence and headed down the river road toward the trees. It was rough going. The wind sent snow devils spinning every which way. It was impossible to see. The new snow was light, but deep and unpacked, so each step I sank in up to my knees. But I had to hurry. Time was passing. Two weeks! The books said it could take as much as two months to get a colt to respond well on lead. I had to get to work. The snow stung as it hit my face, my eyes. I pulled my hat down to protect myself. Maybe if I couldn't teach him to lead I could herd him to the upper pasture, up to the line shack. No, impossible. It would take too long, and I'd have a terrible time. I would have to have another horse to do it, and Grandpa would find out what I was doing then. I just had to get him on lead. I should have brought the halter today. Even if there wasn't room to lead him around in the shed, I could at least be getting him used to it. The horse shed was visible now, a blurry, dark spot not far ahead of me. The wind burned my cheeks and made my eyes water. My nose was dripping. . . . I would just have to wait until tomorrow to work with the halter.

I looked out across the pasture. The sled was nowhere in sight. It was safe to come out of the trees to cross over to the shed.

Only Dancer and the mares were there. They were clustered in one corner, tangled together like tree branches. Dancer's head was crossed over the black mare's neck, and Goldie, Dancer's mother, stood to one side of the black mare with her head across the mare's back.

"Trying to keep warm?" I asked the colt, my breath steaming out in clouds and joining the thick smell of hay and manure in the air. Pal whimpered.

"I wasn't talking to you, silly. I was talking to Dancer."

As I spoke, the colt raised his head from the mare's neck. He listened.

"You recognize your name, don't you?"

His eyes were fastened on me warily, but he hadn't moved away. I stepped closer.

"I brought you some oats today. I should have brought the halter. We have a lot to do," I said, reaching for some oats and moving closer.

Dancer moved to the front of the black mare,

and she turned and walked away from me toward the opposite end of the shed. Goldie and Dancer followed.

"Hey, wait a minute. This is good stuff. You know . . . oats. . . ."

Dancer faced me again. He tossed his mane and lifted his velvet nose to smell my hand and offering. His eyes held me; bright, clear brown, they seemed to be checking me over. Maybe looking to see if there was any sign of that contraption I had put on him the other night.

One hand was stretched toward him with the oats. I held up my other hand. "Look. See. Nothing. I just want to pet you. Maybe pull a burr or two out of your mane, if you'll let me, but I won't try anything. I promise."

The colt snorted, then shook all over. Dust and bits of straw flew into the air around him. He took several steps toward my oat-filled hand. He stopped and pressed his neck forward, trying to reach the oats without coming too close.

"Come on. Come on," I coaxed, "you have to trust me. I'm trying to help you, trying to keep you right here on this ranch where you belong. But you have to know how to act, got to have some training. Your father was very smart and brave, but he didn't know how to act, didn't know his place with people, and he got into real trouble. That's not going to happen to you!"

He took another step. His warm nose touched my hand. The soft, thick winter coat on his belly moved gently with his breath. As he took the oats from one hand, I stole my other forward to touch him, to feel the feathery, red softness of his neck. I stroked him slowly, gently. He munched on the oats. I moved closer, closer, until I was standing beside him. He didn't move. He let me stay. Slowly, I put my face close to his neck and turned my cheek into his warmth. I slid my hand under his neck on one side and rested my cheek on the other. And he let me! He didn't turn around, or jerk away, or anything. He let me hug him as he nuzzled my hand looking for more oats.

"Dancer," I whispered into his fur, "I know you're my horse. I'll show them you're mine. I can train you. I will! We'll show them! I don't need their help. We can do it!"

I was so happy. He was standing with me. I took my now-empty hand away from his mouth and wrapped both arms around his neck.

"Some wild, mean horse! I wish they could see you now."

Just then, Dancer did a side step. He wrenched from my grasp, turned, kicked up his heels, barely missing me, and galloped out of the shed into the snowy pasture. He didn't go far; he turned and made a short, tight circle and galloped back to the shed. He wanted to get back to the mares, I knew. Before he entered the shed, he dropped his head and looked at me. The white blaze of his forehead matched the snow. He lifted his head, tossed back his blond mane, and reared. His front hooves flew menacingly through the air; then, as they smacked down hard on some ice hidden under the snow, he slipped. He spread all four legs to keep his balance. Suddenly, he looked like a gangly puppy on a slippery floor. Quickly, he pulled himself together and walked briskly past me to join the mares. He held his head especially high and proud as if to regain his dignity.

I had to giggle. "Dancer, you don't have to impress me. I know how wonderful you are. It's all right if you stumble sometimes."

He had woven himself in between the mares again and had turned his back to me. I still had a few grains of oats in my pocket. Maybe I could get close to him once more. I was feeling the cold, though, and I still had to walk back up to the house. It would probably be better to go now and come back tomorrow with the halter. Pal came up and rubbed against my leg. He was ready to go. "In a minute, boy." I wished I could hug the colt just one more time . . . to say good-bye.

Clink, clink, clink, clink. . . . A steady rhythm of iron on iron, drawing near the shed. Harness jangling . . . the sled was coming—Grandpa! *Clink, clink. . . .* Louder. I turned and ran out of the shed, Pal beside me.

I didn't look back and I didn't dare stop until I was safely out of sight. Pal was right beside me. We ran deep into the cottonwoods before I finally stopped to rest. I leaned against a tree trunk that was big enough to block the wind and tried to catch my breath. That was a close call. Pal didn't seem tired at all. He went racing off across the snow.

Then. . . .

Whooo, whooo, whooo, whooo, whooo.

The owl! Why was it calling in the day? Where was Pal? I peered through the snowflakes, but saw nothing. The world had gone blank white.

Whooo, whooo, whooo, whooo, whooo. Again.

"Pal!" I shouted. Shielding my eyes with my hands, I looked in the direction that he'd gone. The shadowy trunks of two big trees on either side of me formed archways to an invisible world . . . ice monsters guarding the entrance, their branch-arms arced and pointing twisted twig fingers to the thick white sky. From above me came a crack. A sharp snapping, like a stick breaking over your knee. I turned toward the sound. A huge gray shadow floated like a ghost out of the tree above me.

Startled, I began to run. My legs moved under me, but I couldn't see. My foot hooked on something under the snow, and I tumbled foward.

"Are you hurt?"

I stiffened in surprise, and slowly sat up.

"I'm just fine," I muttered. I wiped the snow from my eyebrows and eyelashes so I could see.

John Yellowfeather stood in front of me, grinning, his eyes filled with laughter. I just knew he was laughing at me. I could feel the snow caked on my face and knew I looked dumb. I wiped my face again and stood up, brushing the snow off my coat.

"What's so funny?" I asked.

"Nothing." He just stood there.

Finally, just to break the silence, I said, "Aren't you John Yellowfeather who went to the Cartersville School?"

"Aren't you Janey Anderson who went to the Cartersville School?" he mimicked, smiling.

I had to smile, too. "If you recognized me, why didn't you say something before?"

"Why didn't you?" he asked, shrugging.

I thought for a moment. "Well, I don't know. I guess I expected you to speak to me . . . or something . . . I don't know. . . ."

There was another long silence. The wind

really stung my wet cheeks. Pal came bounding up. "Where have you been? Off rabbit chasing? I'm freezing. We better get home."

I turned to John Yellowfeather, who was still standing there. "I've got to get back. We've been out a long time."

We began to walk together through the snow. We didn't speak, but strained through the drifts, side by side, leaning into the wind. When we reached the protection of the hill below the barn, I stopped to catch my breath. John stopped, too. I knocked some of the snow off my muffler. He watched me from beneath the visor of his hat. His shoulders were hunched up around his ears and his hands were tucked into the pockets of his big jacket. He had no neck. I thought of an owl. "Did you . . . did you hear that owl calling back in the cottonwoods?" I blurted.

He nodded.

"Isn't it funny that the owl would call in broad daylight?"

John shrugged. "Sometimes they do. Anyway, it's not 'broad' daylight today. More like 'narrow' daylight," he said, looking up into the storm.

My turn to smile. "I never thought of it that way," I said. "Narrow daylight."

"What were you doing out there anyway?" John asked abruptly.

"I wanted to see my colt," I said before I

thought. I shouldn't be telling anyone about it—not if my plan was going to work. That way there was no chance of it getting back to Grandpa. I was trying to think of a way to take back what I had said, when John asked:

"You mean that sorrel in the shed?"

I started.

"Yes," I answered warily. "How do you know about him?"

"He's a nice-looking colt. Real curious. He almost came up to me before."

A burning shot through my chest. "You better stay away from him . . . I mean, be careful, because he doesn't know anyone but me. He's not broken . . . trained. I mean, he's not dangerous or mean, but he's not really tame. He knows me and I'm going to train him . . . but. . . ." I stopped. What was I babbling about? I was telling him everything—because I didn't want Dancer to go up to him. I wanted to be the only person he would trust. He was my colt.

John was looking at me strangely. "Your colt has a wire cut on the inside of his left leg. Not a bad one, but you should keep an eye on it," he said, and, turning quickly, started up the hill alone.

I followed, trying to catch up. I didn't want him to leave like that. I knew I must have hurt his feelings when I told him to stay away from the colt. I didn't mean to be so sharp, but . . .

and he saw a wire cut. I never saw it, but then I hadn't looked for anything like that. I was just excited about touching, hugging the colt. I felt guilty because I hadn't thought about taking care of him that way. I felt jealous that this stranger could almost get up to Dancer—and knew enough to look him over carefully.

When I reached the top of the hill, John was already at the bunkhouse. I ran after him, but he was up the steps quickly. He paused for a moment on the porch, saw me coming, raised his hand in a half-wave and disappeared inside. I slowed to a walk. I climbed up the porch steps. When I opened the back door I could smell the mince pies.

"Janey?" Grandma called.

"Yep, it's me!" I answered.

"Good. I was worried about you. Come on in here. It's lunch time."

Everyone was at the table, including Grandpa. He must have trotted the team all the way to the barn. I sat down at my place across from Greg.

"Where on earth were you, Janey?" Mom asked. "It didn't take you all that time to get the Yellowfeathers settled in. Mr. Yellowfeather was unpacked and off with your Grandpa ages ago."

"Just down in the cottonwoods. It was very pretty."

"Well, it wasn't pretty on that feeding sled, I'll

tell you," Grandpa said. "Couldn't see where I was going. I might have driven over a cow or two for all I know. Hit some big bumps."

He was in a good mood. Things must have gone OK with Tom Yellowfeather.

"Do you think it will clear tomorrow, Henry?" Grandma asked.

"Yep. I think it'll blow out of here by tonight. Tomorrow will be one of them cold, clear suckers. Just can't win in this country. First you get blown off the feed sled, then you get frozen to it if you stand still for more than two seconds at a time. Hard to stay alive at all." He leaned back against his chair and sipped his coffee. "You kids check the woodbin. Make sure it's filled up to the brim. If the old mercury drops as far as I think it will tonight, we're going to need more sticks than usual to keep warm."

No matter how cold it was tomorrow, I'd have to get down to the colt. Only ten more days of vacation to get him in that halter and on lead.

Grandpa was staring at me through the spirals of cigarette smoke he had just blown out through his nose. It made me nervous. My leg began to swing against the bench under the table. Could he read my mind?

"Don't forget about that wood, now, Janey," he said.

"I won't, Grandpa."

82

Progress

The sunlight poured through my windows making the table beside my bed, my chair, and the floor shine like the rocks in the spring basin do when the fresh water washes over them. Suppose, I thought, that the white, thick snow of yesterday was the soap that sudsed the prairie all up, and now it was being rinsed in sunshine. Outside, the world sparkled. The fence posts gleamed where the sun poked at them, showing the diamonds which had been driven into their cracks and gnarls by the wind. Today was beautifully bright and still. Still and clear as fresh ice . . . and probably as cold. It wasn't bad in my room. Mom must have put more wood in the stove during the night. As I rummaged through my drawers looking for a clean undershirt and some fresh long johns, I tried to stand directly in the big, wide stream of sun which burst through my windows. It was so warm on my skin . . . like summer. I couldn't wait to get outside—to get down to the colt.

I ran downstairs. The smell of buckwheat cakes and fresh coffee met me in the hallway.

"There you are," Grandma said. "We've got plans for you today."

"I have my own plans," I said as quickly and politely as I could.

"They will have to wait, at least for an hour or two," Mom piped in. "Greg is going to the mailbox. While he's gone, you can get the frosting mixed."

I started to say something sarcastic about Greg's going to the mailbox, but held my tongue. I had more important business, like how I was going to get out of helping with the cookies.

I turned and looked out the window. Greg was riding Blue through the gate. It made me so mad! I was *really* determined now to get out to the colt. "Grandma, please let me go outside this morning. I promise you I'll decorate those cookies this afternoon."

"Janey, it may look beautiful, but it is about five degrees below zero. It will be warmer for you this afternoon."

"I promise I won't stay out too long, and when I come in I'll do whatever you want me to do."

"Just get the job done now," Grandma said in her "enough-of-this-nonsense" tone.

I stabbed the pancake with my fork. I didn't care one bit for Christmas hustle and bustle this year. Not about the decorations, the baking or the presents. All I could think about was working with the colt. All this Christmas stuff was just wasting what little time I had to train him. I gulped down my pancakes and hurried to get the ingredients for the frosting. I would whip through this job as fast as I could. Through the pantry window, I saw John going along the path to the river. I felt sick. What if he was headed up to see Dancer?

I had the frosting all mixed and had started decorating the cookies before Greg came in carrying the mailbag. His cheeks were fiery red, and he grinned proudly as he handed the dirty canvas bag to Grandma.

"I did it. The mailbox door was frozen and I had to get down off the horse to bang it open. . . . Then I took old Blue over to the gate and climbed up on the gate so I could get back up on him all by myself. Isn't that good?" He was beaming.

"That's terrific. You can tell Grandpa all about it when he gets back from feeding . . . and

Daddy will be so proud when you tell him on Friday," Mom said, hugging him.

He looked over at me so happily. I had to say something. "That's very good, Greg." I meant it, too. I remembered how wonderful it felt to be able to do that sort of thing alone when you were his age. But I was still a little jealous.

While Mom and Grandma went over the newspaper which had come in the mail and read the Christmas cards, Greg and I worked on the cookies. We did a pretty messy job, but I just wanted to get done. Finally we finished.

It wasn't hard to smuggle the halter outside. I put it inside my shirt and covered it with two sweaters. Once outside, I hurried to the granary and filled my pockets with oats. I wanted everything to go smoothly today. Just as I was ready to go out through the barn and down the hill to the horse shed, Grandpa and Tom Yellowfeather pulled into the yard with the feeding sled. I ducked down and hurried along the back of the corral.

When I was in full cover of the cottonwood trees, I stopped, undid my coat, and pulled the halter out from under my sweaters. I felt much more comfortable with it hanging on my shoulder. Even in the deep snow, it didn't seem to take long to get to the horse shed. My route was direct except where I detoured around the deer carcass. I felt spooky about that place.

I came out of the cottonwoods on the edge of the pasture and looked around for the colt. The mares were over by the salt lick, and Smoky was next to the shed. Then I saw him! Standing in the sunlight, his coat glistening red, he held his head proudly as a young buck deer balancing a crown of antlers. He seemed magical, like a fairy tale creature, too powerful for plain people. How could I possibly think I could halter or tame him?

He trotted across the trampled snow of the pasture toward me and drew quite close before he stopped. I reached into my pocket and drew out a mittenful of oats. I extended my arm. He stretched his neck and sniffed at my hand, not touching me, just sniffing. I saw the wire cut John was talking about. His hair was torn away, and there was a long scab on the inside of his left rear leg, but it didn't look bad, just a scratch. I was relieved.

"Come on," I coaxed, and tried to cluck to him with my tongue. He took another step, the white blaze down his nose catching the sun as he reached toward the oats. I felt the weight of the halter on my shoulder. So far, so good. At last he dropped his muzzle into my hand and began to munch on the oats. I stepped closer to him, and let the halter slide down from my shoulder and into my hand.

Now how could I maneuver the halter around without frightening him? I tried to lift it, but didn't get very far because I was standing on the lead rope. Stupid! Then I saw the halter was tangled. I was going to have to use two hands. I tried slowly moving the oat hand away so I could straighten out the halter. The colt stepped back quickly.

"Wait a minute. I've got more of those oats. Just wait a minute."

I took the halter in both hands and slowly approached him again. He shook his mane off his forehead and backed up. I reached in my pocket and got more oats. How was I going to do this? To get him to stand still, I needed the oats, but I had to have both hands to put the halter on him. Why didn't I think to bring a bucket? Then I had an idea. I could put oats in my hat and put my hat down in front of him. While he ate out of my hat, I could get the halter on.

I tried that. The colt watched me as I placed my hat on the snow in front of him. He sniffed at the hat curiously. He went after the oats right away, but only with a nibble. I wanted to wait until he had a big mouthful before I tried anything. He reached down into the hat again, only this time he picked up the hat, too. The oats spilled out into the snow, and he took several inquisitive chaws of my hat before spitting it out. Now what?

I would just have to try to get the halter on him without the oats. I walked up slowly and patted him gently on the neck. He didn't jump away. He knew he was my horse! He'd let me put a halter on him in the middle of the night and let me hug him yesterday. . . . Now he was standing quite still in the middle of an open pasture letting me do it again! I took a deep breath, then slowly I reached up behind his ears and began to scratch as I had that night. Carefully, I slid the rope around his nose and stood on tiptoes to bring it up behind his ears.

Suddenly, the white streak on his nose flew up past my face into the sky. I scrambled backward as his front hooves rose off the snow and pawed the air before they landed again, very close to me. The colt whinnied and kicked out his hind legs as though they were detached from the front part of his body. He arched his back as his hooves hit the snow. He made a stiff-legged buck, then galloped out to the fence and back again to the horse shed. There he stopped and looked at me as if he were saying, "See! I win!"

I picked up a hunk of snow and threw it as hard as I could into a drift. "Darn it," I screamed at the colt. "Don't you know I'm trying to help you?" He stood very calm and princely beside the shed. I could feel the veins throbbing in my forehead.

Pal came running up. He gave a short bark. I turned around. There, leaning against the trunk of a cottonwood, was John Yellowfeather, grinning at me again.

"Ohhh!" I groaned. I wanted to throw something at *him*, now. "Don't laugh! I'm having a tough enough time," I snapped.

John was silent for a moment, then shrugged and started to walk away.

"Wait," I called.

He turned.

"I . . . I . . . well, could you maybe help me with this halter?"

"Yesterday you told me to stay away from your colt."

"I told you that because . . . well, I didn't want you to get hurt." I tried to sound nonchalant. "After you told me about his cut, I figured you knew about horses."

John looked at me curiously. "Why are you doing it alone?"

"Because he's my colt. I *want* to do it myself," I answered. "*Do* you know anything about horses?"

John only nodded, then asked to see the halter. He examined it carefully and handed it back to me. "Good. My uncle has some like that. He breaks horses for ranchers up at the reservation. He has a string of rodeo buckers, too. I help him with them sometimes."

"Well, it won't be any trouble for you to help me with this then," I said quickly. "I've been having a little trouble with him alone, but he's not a bucker, or anything like that. And he knows me. I've been around him since he was born. I've got some oats, so we can catch him, because he'll come right up and eat out of my hand. Come on, I'll show you. I'll get him to come up to me, and you help me get the halter on him so I can start him on lead. OK? I know I can handle him alone once I get this halter on."

"You talk faster than that colt can run," John said, raising one eyebrow up under the dark swatch of hair that fell across his forehead.

For a moment I was afraid he wasn't going to help me, but then he walked over and together we started across the pasture toward the colt.

"Try to walk him up into that corner," John said, and raised his chin slightly to point toward the corner of the barbed wire fence. I moved out to the left so we could turn the colt in that direction. We came in pretty close on him before he turned and began walking briskly right where we wanted him to go. He stopped as he neared the fence.

"Let me have the halter," John said, watching the colt and holding out his hand. I placed the halter in it and waited for the next order. "Stay behind me," he said, staring intently at the colt.

The colt tossed his head and lifted his nose into the air. He sniffed, then dropped it down to the snow. Suddenly he lifted his head with a jerk and turned toward the fence on his right.

"Move up," John said calmly. "Don't crowd him, but keep him in the corner. We have him. You can give him the oats in a minute, but we need him in that corner. . . . If he tries running at you, don't back down. He'll stop."

"Don't back down." The words rang in my ears. That's what Grandpa had said to me before he went out to bring in the stallion. "If he runs at you, keep that bola going, and don't back down!"

A short, blasting whinny broke the silence as the colt went back on his hind legs and pivoted. Maybe John was going to be as tough with Dancer as Grandpa had been with the stallion?

"Hold it there, little horse," John said, lifting the halter in front of him. "Just stay right there."

He was speaking gently as we moved closer. The colt watched warily. John motioned for me to stop. He moved a step closer. Then another. He was standing next to the colt. Slowly, he reached forward with his right hand. He did not touch the colt, but ran his hand through the air inches in front of the colt's face . . . past the white blaze, over the top of his ears. He made a slow, easy circle with his bare hand around the horse's neck and back again. The colt was quite still. John repeated the movements, his hand not touching, not coming any closer than before, but moving slowly, hypnotically. John was still except for his floating hand. He didn't lift the halter, just passed his hand slowly through the air around the colt's head. Now, just as slowly, he began to lift the halter. He didn't speak, but made some soft, humming, pigeonlike sound as he lifted the halter higher and higher. He took the top of the halter in both hands . . . then it was on the colt's head. I didn't even see how he did it. Just as quickly, he fastened the snap. The halter was on!

The colt gave his head a slight toss, as if he didn't believe that new feeling was attached in any way and he could casually get rid of it. When he found it didn't go away that easily, he lowered his head, all four legs braced stiffly, and shook so hard his mane flew out about him like straw in a windstorm. The lead rope, which John held securely with both hands, wiggled and jumped through the air. John was holding on to it, though, and moving up on it, hand over hand.

The colt threw his head back and stopped the shaking. He stood very still. John came in closer, slowly coiling the rope, shortening the lead. The colt started walking away, but as he felt the pressure, the firm hold on his freedom, he stopped. He looked back at us. Then he was up on his back legs, his front hooves striking at the rope. John leaned back, putting his weight against it.

"Get over here. Get your weight on the back of this rope. Hurry!" he shouted.

I ran up behind him and grabbed the end of the rope. Just as I was tightening my grip there was a big jerk, and I lurched forward. The rope began to slide through my hands. I grabbed and tried to pull it tighter. John dug his feet into the snow and was pulling back with all his weight. The colt was facing us, twisting and turning, making little bucks, swinging his head from side to side, bracing all four legs and pulling back on the lead. He gained ground. John was sliding through the snow, his heels plowing a path. "Dig in! Dig in!" John yelled.

I leaned back with all my might. The colt was dragging us both slowly through the snow . . . then he stopped.

"Hold on, now. Hold him!" John said, as he began moving hand over hand forward. The colt jumped to the side. He kicked and reared. John was jerked off balance. The colt, feeling the slackening pressure, broke out. I was holding on to the end of the lead. The knot there was almost jerked through my hands. John tried to brace his feet in the snow, but was pulled forward again. He ran a few steps with the colt, then stumbled on a block of frozen snow and fell. He lay on his belly in the snow, holding the rope as I was dragged toward him. He was skidding across the snow on his belly. I threw my weight into the rope. I dug my heels in as the end knot pulled and tore at my hands.

The colt stopped. He looked back at us, then, nose to the ground, began to twist his head from side to side, leaning back onto his haunches, matching his weight to ours. John jumped to his feet and began moving up to the colt again. I leaned back with all the strength I could muster. John was closer, closer. Then he was there. He had his hand on the rope right up under the colt's chin. The colt lifted his head. His eyes rolled wildly. White showed all the way around the dark center. John jerked down on the ring under the colt's chin. The colt looked surprised, almost docile, but only for a moment. He pulled his head back, shaking it, jerking it. My arms were being dragged out of the sockets. John was being jerked and tossed every which way; still he gripped the halter. Then the colt stopped. His sides were heaving. The trampled snow lay about us as testimony to his fight, but no more flew out from his digging, kicking hooves.

We all stood warily watching each other. John took hold of the ring on the halter under the colt's chin. He held tightly to the lead rope and placed his foot forward. He pulled against the lead rope. I did the same. The colt moved with us . . . one step, two steps. He was following. Another step. Each step was pulled, but each step was made. He was going our way. Just as I thought we were ready to start really walking him, John motioned for me to halt. I pulled up the little slack there was in the rope. John told me to ease it again, then he reached up and unsnapped the halter.

"What are you doing? What are you doing? Don't let him go now. We only just got him going," I shouted.

But the halter was off. The colt, no longer feeling any constriction, spun on his hind legs and ran like a racehorse out into the pasture, sending explosions of snow out behind his hooves.

"Why did you untie him?" I yelled indignantly. "We were only just getting somewhere. We had him started! I knew I shouldn't have let you help. I should have done it alone."

John stared at me, puzzled at first, then his eyes grew dark. He threw the halter at my feet and started toward the cottonwoods. I called after him, but he didn't turn around. He charged on, head down, toward the bare trees.

I ran after him. "Wait a minute. Will you wait a minute?" I ran as fast as I could and caught up to him. He wouldn't turn around. He wouldn't look at me. "Wait. . . ." I reached out and caught the arm of his jacket. He shook me off and kept going. "I'm sorry," I said. He walked on. "I said I'm sorry!" I yelled this time, running behind him again. "I was really stupid to yell like that before, but will you tell me why you let him go?" I asked more quietly as I tried to keep up with him.

"You *asked* me to help—you didn't *let* me." He shook his head. "Don't you know anything? Couldn't you tell he was resting, getting his steam up to start again? We wouldn't have been able to hold him. He would have wrapped us in the barbed wire." John turned and looked right at me. "Why did you tell me he was a barnyard colt? Maybe he let you touch him, but he doesn't know people. And you don't know horses! You're lucky he didn't get you in the head with those front hooves before now."

He turned away and headed for the trees.

"John, wait!" I called. "I'm sorry. I want to talk to you."

He slowed down, but didn't wait. I hurried to

catch up, but stumbled on a dead branch hidden in the snow and fell. John kept going.

"Darn it," I hissed as I scrambled up. "I told him I was sorry. Ohhhh, what a mess!" I flung the lead rope out like a whip and lashed at a tree trunk. The snow, which had been driven into the crevices in the bark during yesterday's storm, leaped out in a flurry of icy chunks. One piece crossed the space between John and me and plunked him on the back of the head. *Whup!*

John wheeled and glared at me. He looked furious.

"I didn't throw that," I stammered.

"What did you do, kick it?" he snapped.

"No, I did not. It came off the tree trunk when I . . ."

"Sure, sure it did. And that colt is real tame and knows you. Why are you following me?"

I didn't say anything. A tree limb squeaked a frozen protest into the silence between us as the wind leaned against it. It was the first I was aware of the wind that had come up. Through the tangle of winter-bare branches, I could see the glare of the sun was gone, too. The sky was chalky, and it was growing colder. I could feel a chunk of snow lodged inside the cuff of my coat. John glowered at me like an angry teacher determined to make me give the right answer. I wiggled my hand around, trying to get the snow out of my cuff. I didn't know what to say. Pal whimpered and rubbed his head against my leg. He had stayed so far from the struggle with the colt, I had practically forgotten about him. I shivered from the cold. John stared at me for a moment more, then slowly, reluctantly, a grin spread across his face.

"You are crazy. You would rather freeze to death than answer a question, wouldn't you?"

I nodded.

John looked down. He kicked at a clump of sage. "Come on," he said, waiting while I caught up to him.

The trees moaned and complained in the wind. Frost and snow blew off their branches and floated through the air, flat and shiny.

Pal growled low and long. He stopped walking with us and moved to the side, his lips curled back over his teeth, his growl more threatening. There, in a small clearing, the pointed hoof jutted upward out of the snow. The flesh was stripped, now, from the leg beneath it. John walked over to the half-eaten carcass.

"A doe," he said.

"I know. Coyotes got her," I said.

He looked at me, his head tilted to the side quizzically. "How do you know it was coyotes?"

"I saw them. I was down here a couple of nights ago when they brought her down."

John didn't seem to know whether he should believe me or not. "How many of them did it?"

"I only saw four, but it was dark and snowing. There could have been more."

"What were you doing down here prowling around with coyotes?"

At least I had someone I could tell now. "I was trying to get a halter on the colt."

"By yourself? At night? Why?"

"Because I thought I could sneak up on him while he was sleeping," I said sarcastically.

"But the coyotes woke him up, right?"

I nodded, making my eyes as big and innocent as I could.

"Come on, tell me," he said and punched me on the shoulder. I pretended to stagger with the blow.

We had been moving along between the trees all this time. Suddenly John stopped. He walked over to a stump, a big cottonwood stump. It was jagged and hollowed. It appeared that the tree had been struck by lightning and killed; then the wind had toppled it, but it was still connected at its base. The snow-covered mounds and bumps made by the dead branches reached way out from the stump. John kicked at the snow piled between the stump and the fallen tree. When there was an opening, he bent down and hollowed it with his hands, making it bigger and wider. Then he crawled into the hole. For a moment, he completely disappeared, then he stuck his head out of the entry. "Come in here out of the wind, and you can tell me the whole story of the sleeping colt and the coyotes."

I crouched down and looked through the hole. John was sitting inside a hollow which was made in the triangle between the tree trunk and the tree. The snow had piled up on either side, but left a bare spot right under the trunk itself. It was a snow house with snow walls, and the trunk of the fallen tree was the roof. I crawled into it. John moved over and made room for me to lean back against the stump. It was warmer out of the wind. When I had settled back he said, "So? What were you doing down here at night?"

For some reason, probably because he'd helped me, I decided to tell him everything. "I was down here at night because I'm trying to halter-break the colt by myself and I'm not supposed to be messing around with him at all. I lied. He isn't mine. He should be, but he isn't. He belongs to my grandpa, and Grandpa's going to sell him . . . because my dad says he has to. What I'm going to do is get him on lead and take him way out in the upper pasture across the river. There's emergency hay there, so he'll have food.

He can winter there. Grandpa won't know where he is and he won't be able to take him to the auction after Christmas."

"Wait a minute! You're going to hide the colt from them?"

"Uh huh."

"But that's stealing. . . ."

I thought about that for a moment. "No, not in the family. It wouldn't be stealing if you're in the same family. And I'm not changing the brand. Besides, he *should* be my colt. They're only selling him because they're mad at each other, Daddy and Grandpa, I mean. Daddy says it's because they don't have enough hay to winter him, but that's just an excuse. They think he's got bad blood, that he's too wild. They said I can have a different horse, later. They just don't want me to have *him*."

"Why do you want this colt so much?"

"I found him when he was first born."

"You'd come out in the middle of the night to try to halter-break a wild colt just because you found him?"

"No, that's not the only reason. His father was the most beautiful stallion I've ever seen. He looks a whole lot like his father."

"Where is the stallion?"

"He's gone. He didn't belong to us. We were just pasturing him for a rancher down in Wyoming. He came here when he was a colt. Grew up in the pastures . . . no one branded him or anything. We had to take him off the ranch. My Grandpa and I drove him down here to the corrals. He fought us all the way, rearing and kicking, biting at our horses. He was plumb crazy-wild."

John smiled. "I've seen those old stallions when you try to break them away from their mares. Bet he scared you a little, didn't he?"

"Yeah, I was a little scared," I said, not admitting I had been terrified. "But you would have been, too, I'll bet."

John tilted his head to the side and shrugged. "Maybe yes, maybe no. Is that the end of the story? You got scared bringing in the stallion and you found the colt?"

"Not exactly."

"I'm listening."

"The stallion was so wild and he had such a strong heart, that after they got him into the corral they couldn't load him in the truck. He reared up and threw himself over backward in the chute. My uncle and my grandpa had to pull him out with ropes and another horse. Then they locked him up in the barn. Grandpa figured if he was in there in the dark for a day or so without food or water, he'd calm down fast. Well, the stallion kicked holes in the side of the barn. Then

Grandpa and my uncle brought him out and tied a log chain to his neck . . . one about this big." I made a circle with my fingers to show how large and heavy each link of the chain had been. "Then they fastened a hunk of cottonwood log to it. Fixed it where it would dangle down and hit his legs as he tried to walk."

John whistled and shook his head.

"The stallion still managed to get across the river with it. He crossed the river twice and was crossing for a third time, when he gave out. He was heading back up to his mares, but he couldn't make it. He was beaten. Grandpa pulled him out of the river, but he wasn't the same horse. It was like he had let his heart die there in the river, and they pulled out the body. Do you know what I mean?"

I looked at John. He was looking down at his boots, but I could tell he was listening to me. Suddenly, I wanted more than anything to have him understand what I felt about the stallion. No one else had. I'd tried to explain to Daddy because he understood most things, but he'd been so worried about business and money, and then his heart attack came. Grandpa only cared about beating the horse . . . being the boss.

He didn't respond, only shifted his gaze to the snow wall opposite us. I waited. When he didn't say anything, I was embarrassed. I should have known better than to try to explain, but I'd gone this far . . . I decided to finish the story.

"Anyway, the day they loaded up the stallion and took him off the ranch, I found the colt. I found him standing out in the pasture looking at me, that lightning blaze down his nose—just like the stallion. . . . I thought that meant something special. I knew he belonged to me."

I stopped. I felt the tears welling up inside my throat. In a minute, I was going to be crying, right there in front of John. I pushed my lips together to hold it down.

"I know what you're talking about," John said, still staring into the snow wall. "About the stallion giving up something in the river. I've seen that happen before . . . to horses . . . to people. Do you know what happened to the stallion after they took him off the ranch?"

"No."

"Sometimes they come back again. They get some life again. They aren't the same as before . . . because they've learned . . . but they find some life."

I was glad I'd told him. He understood a lot. We sat in silence for a time.

"John, what were you doing when you passed your hand in front of the colt? I mean, when you were moving it around in the air in front of him?"

"I was letting him feel me," he answered.

"What? What do you mean?"

"Well, if you were in your house and a stray dog came in the door and he came right up to you and put his open mouth around your arm, you'd try to run, wouldn't you?"

"Yeah, I probably would."

"But if the dog came in and stood and wagged his tail for a minute, maybe wiggled around for a little bit, you'd get to know he was not going to hurt you. Then he could come up and put his mouth on your hand and you wouldn't run. That colt is just like you are. He needs to feel you. . . . You breathe deep and slow and make yourself calm and move your hand around him so he can tell you're calm, then he's not afraid."

"I've been reading a lot about training horses, but I never heard of that."

"There's plenty you can't get from books!" John said, his voice cold and pointed like an icicle.

There was another long silence. Finally, I said, "I have to get back up to the ranch house. If I'm too late, Grandpa will be mad."

"Your grandpa must get mad all the time. You talk about it enough."

"Yes, he gets mad a lot."

"He doesn't like us, does he," John stated more than asked.

Had Grandpa said or done something to Mr.

Yellowfeather? My cheeks burned. I didn't know what to say. "Yes, he does. I mean, he doesn't even know you, but when he does, it will be. . . . Grandpa has a bad temper. He doesn't mean most of what he says. . . . and, well, I'm sorry."

"Don't you be sorry! Not for me . . . not for my father or my mother either! We do fine!" The words hissed out of him, then he sat back and was silent.

Moments passed. John leaned over and looked out the entrance. "We better be getting out of here," he said. The discussion was ended.

We crawled out of the hollow. Out through the trees, on the edge of the hill, the sky was growing dusty lavender, like faded lilac blossoms. I knew I should hurry home, but I didn't want to. I wanted to straighten things out. I liked him . . . and I didn't have much time. He did know about horses, and he could help me with Dancer now. Maybe doing it all alone wasn't as important as getting the job done. . . . It wasn't. Dancer was *my* horse, regardless. John wouldn't even be around come summer. I decided to ask him if we could meet tomorrow to work with the colt. I turned to speak.

He put his finger to his lips to silence me, then he cupped a hand to his ear and pointed at me. I listened, but I heard nothing, only the wind.

"Did you hear it?" he whispered.

I shook my head. He took hold of both ears, held them out to the sides and closed his eyes tightly as though he were in deep concentration. I grinned at his pantomime and listened again. Nothing. I was about to give up when I heard a long, soft sighing riding on the wind.

Whooo, whooo, whooo, whooo, whooo. Five times it sounded, growing louder until it seemed as though the wind had been gathered out of the treetops and pushed through a tunnel. I turned toward the sound. The nightmarish memories shook me. I wanted to run but stopped myself. I moved closer to John. He was looking up into the highest branches of the snow-dusted cotton-woods. He put his finger to his lips and walked a few steps away from our dead tree. He scanned the tree above us and the one next to it. He walked in the opposite direction and stopped. He stared up into a very tall cottonwood. Slowly, carefully, he walked around the trunk, looking up. He stopped. He motioned me forward with a wave of his arm. I took a step. There was a loud crack as my foot struck a dead branch lying fro-zen and brittle under the snow. John turned quickly, narrowed his lips, raised his arms and, with fingers outspread, moved his hands up and down as though he were patting the cold air be-neath them. I nodded to show I had understood. He turned and looked up between the branches

again. I came up beside him. He pointed through
the maze of bare limbs. I couldn't see anything
unusual. When he turned to me with an expec-
tant look, I shook my head. He moved closer to
me and pointed again, his hand level with my
eyes. I still saw nothing except the gray and
brown of the tree bark. I shook my head again.
He raised his eyebrows and shrugged his shoulders in mock exasperation. Then, he put one
hand on my forehead and one on my chin. He
turned my head upward, adjusted it to the left,
and held it. I couldn't move at all. I felt stupid.

"Next to the trunk," he whispered in my ear.

I stared into the branches. My feet were cold
and my nose wanted to run. I was about to tell
him to let me go when I saw something move. I
focused on the spot. The biggest bird I had ever
seen was staring down at us through large yellow eyes. Its head swiveled smoothly from side
to side as though observing each of us carefully,
separately. It was an owl. I'd never seen one
that big. Each eye was rimmed with rust-colored
feathers. A white *V* was drawn from its beak out
to the tufts of black and brown which stood out
on either side of its head like decorations. The
breast was creamy white with scalloped lines of
black running across it. The bird gripped the
branch on which it sat with sharp, curved talons
of black thrust from white-feathered feet. Sud-

denly it sounded again. Five times. Five long wind sounds. I felt tingles inside me, all over me, like sparklers in the dark on the Fourth of July. I looked at John.

"Horned owl. Great big one," he whispered softly. As he spoke, there was a rustling in the branches above us. I looked up just in time to see the owl push off his perch. He extended his huge wings, moving them like giant kites against the air. He climbed upward through the tree-tops. His silhouette, the shadow which had spooked me so when I was alone yesterday, rose high into the twilight of the December afternoon, then began to descend again. The arced wings of the owl were spread wide as it tilted and circled, balancing on the wind. Downward it floated. John and I watched its descent, hypnotized. It passed by the branch of the tree on which it had been perched. Down, down, down. I could see the individual feathers of its outspread tail. Faster it came. Closer, closer. The point of its hooked beak was closer, clear. I threw my hand over my eyes and grabbed for John's hand with the other. There was a muffled *whoosh*, like the sound sheets make when the wind flaps them on the clothesline. Then silence. I remained very still. I felt John's hand leave mine, then he pulled my other hand from my eyes.

"It's OK now. He has gone home again. He

only wanted to say hello. You got scared, didn't you? And you told me you trailed a wild stallion." He shook his head.

I was embarrassed . . . then I remembered the feeling of my hand being squeezed very tightly by his when the owl swooped near us. "Don't give me that. I felt you squeeze my hand. You were frightened, too."

"Only surprised," he insisted, then. . . . "Look, look!" John pointed up into the tree.

The owl had taken his place on the same branch of the cottonwood once again. When John spoke, the owl's beak parted and the sound came once more. I trembled inside. The huge eyes stared as the head tilted downward. John took my hand and squeezed, making his eyes wide with exaggerated fear. He wiggled his knees in pretend tremors. I started laughing. The owl stayed up on his perch watching us. It was growing dark now.

"I have to go home," I said.

"Come on, then." John started across the snow, then he stopped and waved up at the owl. We turned together and headed for the hill below the barn. It wasn't until we were in the yard that I remembered I had left the halter down in the snow house. I told John.

"That's fine. We can pick it up there when we go to work the colt tomorrow," he said.

I was shocked. I hadn't even asked him. "You'll help me again? Even though the colt is pretty wild, you'll try again? Even though . . ." I was going to say something about Grandpa, but stopped myself.

"It's OK," John answered.

John's mother was going from the woodpile to the bunkhouse. She stopped when she saw us.

"I'll see you tomorrow," he said, and ran across the yard. As he reached the bunkhouse, I heard her speak sharply in Cheyenne, her voice crackling through the crisp evening.

I ran the rest of the way to the house.

"Janey, we can't seem to let you out of the house and trust you to come home before you worry us half to death," Grandma fussed as I entered the kitchen.

"Look what I did, Janey," Greg said before Grandma could ask me where I had been. He was over in the corner standing proudly beside an elaborate system of roads laid out on the floor with matchstick boundaries and buildings of boxes beside them. His cars were driving all around it. "Well, what do you think?"

"It's very nice, Greg," I answered absent-mindedly. I had much more important things on my mind.

"Nice? It's terrific and great!" he shouted, and spread his arms into the air over his head.

"OK! It's terrific and great!" I laughed. I wondered if I had thought such simple things terrific and great when I was his age.

Grandpa came in, and Mom told us to sit down for supper.

"How did the feeding go today, Henry?" Grandma asked.

"Went fine. Had a little trouble chopping out one of the water holes. That ice is tricky this year. It's been cold enough so that it's frozen solid next to the bank, but when you go out far enough to get water, the ice is spotty. Thick some places, thin in others. Old Yellowfeather went through today. Wasn't deep, but he got his pant legs wet, and his boots. Damn cold. We had to hightail it up here so he could change before we finished feeding."

"How is he doing?" Mom asked timidly.

"So far he's doing the work," Grandpa said.

Grandma turned to me. "Janey, you haven't even tried the sled or your skates out, yet. You realize it's only two days until Christmas Eve? Time is flying."

"I thought I might take my skates down to that good place by the old river crossing tomorrow. The water isn't deep there, so the ice should be frozen way down. It should be safe. I'll just have to clean it off some." I had my excuse to get out of the house tomorrow!

"Greg will help you. He should get outside," Mom said.

I gulped. I couldn't do anything if Greg came along. He'd tell. He'd ruin everything.

"I don't want to go ice skating. It's too cold. I froze going to the mailbox today. Besides, I want to play with my highways and cars," Greg said as he got up from the table.

I waited for Mom to insist, but she didn't. I breathed a silent sigh of relief. Everyone was in a good mood tonight. After supper, I cleared the table without being asked and dried the dishes, too. I couldn't wait until tomorrow.

Misery and Mystery

My arms were stiff and sore from the punishment they had taken on the end of the lead rope the day before, but I didn't let that slow me down. I got dressed and downstairs before Grandpa had gone out to feed. If there was work I had to do around the house, I wanted to get it over with so I would be free by midmorning when Grandpa finished up in the pasture.

I helped with the breakfast dishes and got out the stuff Grandma needed to make bread. Then she had me go outside and around to the root cellar to bring up the roast for the Christmas Eve dinner. She wanted to thaw it slowly today, so it would be ready to season and pop in the oven tomorrow. I had to wipe the snow off the slanting door to the root cellar before I could open it. It reminded me of the snow house in the cottonwoods . . . and the halter. I looked around the yard. There was no sign of John. We hadn't made any specific plans to meet. I didn't want to go ask for him at the bunkhouse. Maybe he would come out when Grandpa and his father returned.

When they did, the clouds were gathering over the big bluff. It was certain to snow before the afternoon was over. I wanted to get started with the colt as soon as I could.

"If you don't have anything more for me to do, I think I'll go skating now," I said, trying to sound causal.

"Why don't you wait until we have a little lunch?"

"No, I think it might snow. I want to have some . . . skating time before it does."

"You are the limit, child. You have been wandering around outside by yourself ever since you got here," Grandma laughed.

" 'Bye," I called as I went out the back door. Then I remembered I was supposed to be going skating. I ran back in and got my skates.

John wasn't in the yard. I decided to go down the river road and cut through the trees to the snow house. Maybe he would meet me there. I had to get the halter, anyway.

I hurried through the snow, following my path of yesterday. You could go a lot faster where the snow was packed. When I reached the dead doe, I knew I had gone too far and missed the snow house. I backtracked. The snow house was undisturbed. The lead rope was trailing out the entrance. I reached down to pick it up. Just as I grabbed the rope, it was jerked from my hand. Or I thought it was. Maybe I dropped it. I was still a little spooked down here alone. I picked it up again and tried to pull it. This time, it wouldn't move. I jerked again. It jerked back. I leaned down and looked into the opening. John sat holding the halter. He burst into laughter at the sight of me.

"Real funny! Here, you take these," I said handing him my skates, "and I'll take that halter. I'm supposed to be ice skating. Are you ready?" I asked as he tucked my skates back in the house.

"Yeah, I got an idea, too. Did you bring some oats?"

I shook my head. "I forgot."

"Well, we will have to get along without them. I want to get him haltered up by the shed. Then we can fasten a lead rope to a corner pole—use it like a snubbing post—and let him jerk around on that instead of pulling us to pieces like he did yesterday. If we had some oats, we might bribe him to stay calm, but. . . ."

We were walking across the pasture now. John looked over at me. "Did you name the colt?"

"Yes. Fire Dancer."

John laughed. "That's too highfalutin' for a range horse."

His laughter irritated me. Maybe the name really wasn't right for this strong, winter-rough colt we were going after. But still, I was used to him as Dancer.

"Well," I said defensively, "I call him Dancer for short."

He thought for a moment, then said, "It's not a bad name, but it's not his name. He needs something . . . stronger."

Just then the colt poked his head around the side of the shed, as though he knew we were talking about him.

"Look at that. He's just waiting for his lesson. So here we go again." John reached over and took the halter from me.

The colt backed up into the shed. John followed him. He motioned for me to stay back. "Be ready to run to either side of the opening here.

Head him off. Keep him in the shed," John said, his voice low and calm.

As he walked toward the colt, my heart pounded as though it were going to come through my jacket. I wanted so much for the colt to learn to be led, but I was afraid. John was right. He wasn't a barnyard colt. He was a wild thing even though he let me walk up to him. Today, he didn't seem to want to allow even that. He marched back and forth in the shed, weaving through the mares and Smoky, his head swinging from side to side. He snorted and tossed his mane as if to warn John when he got too close. I stood on the open side of the three-walled shed hoping I could stop him if he tried to get out. This went on and on. Then John got him back in a corner alone. John started purring to him, lifting his hand slowly, then letting it drop to the side. The halter he held low behind him, out of sight.

The colt calmed down, stood quietly. John lifted the halter and had it on in seconds. As the colt tossed his head lightly, John fastened it. Then he took the lead rope and backed off a few feet. He made clicking noises. The colt listened, then dropped his head to the floor of the shed, all four legs spread out. He threw his head up, jerking back on the rope. John let him have some slack, then took it up again. John walked backward, toward the outside corner of the shed. He urged the colt with him, step by step. I didn't know what I could do to help. I stayed back and watched. The colt came forward, not resisting. One, two, three, four steps. John stopped at the corner. He quickly made two wraps around the corner support pole with the lead rope and threw on a knot of some kind to fasten it. Then John stepped back. The colt moved forward slowly, as though not certain of his footing. He walked past the corner of the shed. He started into the pasture, but was stopped by the rope.

Suddenly his rear end flew out in a kick filled with fury. He lashed out again with his hind legs. He slipped as they landed and fell into the snow, but was up again in a flurry of snow and mane. He twisted his head from side to side. He tried to rear, but he was jerked back down by the lead. The other horses trotted out of the shed, snorting and tossing heads as though they smelled a storm coming. The sound of their hooves on the packed snow seemed to inflame the colt more. He kicked and arched and bucked. He lashed out at the rope with his front hooves. I was terrified. What if he hurt himself?

"Stop him!" I shouted to John. "He's gone crazy. He's going to get hurt."

Skkkkkkkkrrrrrraccck! The sound of splintering wood cut through the thudding of the colt's hooves and my shouts. I looked at the post. John was racing toward it. The corner post was being ripped away from the cottonwood beam on top of it. The whole roof was going to cave in! John ran between the colt and the post. The colt hit at him with a hoof. John dodged it and reached for the fastener to the halter. He almost had it, but the colt swung his head and it was wrenched from John's hands. *Skkkkrrrrack!*

"Get outside!" John managed to shout at me as he tried again to reach the snap fastener.

I couldn't move. I stood petrified. Then the colt swung his head to the side and the halter came off. He galloped out into the field and didn't stop to look back. John had somehow gotten it unfastened. The empty halter lay on the ground; the lead rope was still tied to the post. John looked up at the beam and pointed to the place where it had split around the nail which held it to the corner post.

"That wood was rotten. I didn't bargain for that. Narrow escape!" John said shaking his head. "How would you explain that one to your grandpa? If it had fallen now . . . if the whole roof had caved in, you would have been in serious trouble. Now you can wait for a while, then tell him you think the shed needs some work, and he will think you are pretty smart."

I didn't answer. I couldn't.

"Are you OK?" John asked.

I nodded.

"He's a tough horse. Not mean. He didn't go after us, didn't try to hurt us, but he's tough. I don't think we can train him in a few days. We need a corral with a deep-set snubbing post. He's going to have to work some of the devil out before he's ready to work with you. I'm sorry, but I think that's what we need."

I turned and walked off. I didn't want him to see me crying. For the first time since the colt was born, I felt he wasn't mine, that there was more to having him than just wanting him. I heard John's footsteps behind me, but I didn't look back. I walked on to the snow house and crawled inside. I leaned against the stump and drew my knees up to my chest. I wasn't crying. I felt empty.

"Can I come in?"

Before I could answer, John was in and sitting beside me. We were silent for some time.

"At least the colt has a name now," John said.

"What?"

"Wrecker," he said without a smile.

"That's a terrible name!" I protested.

"Not so bad. It's strong. The word sounds good—*rek-ker*. That's it. Just spell it like it sounds. R-E-K-K-E-R."

It doesn't matter what he's called," I said numbly. "He isn't mine. Grandpa is going to sell him." I stated it simply. It wasn't so hard to say it.

Silence again.

Finally John spoke. "Sometimes these things turn out for the best. . . . I know that sounds dumb, but it's true. I mean it happened to me. Not just like this, but pretty bad. Then something happened and I was glad for the way things went."

"What happened?"

John stared at me. "It's not important now," he answered softly.

Suddenly there was a *shhhhhh* from high in the branches over our heads. We both looked up. The great horned owl was settling on a branch, his wings outstretched, gently moving to balance himself as he shifted his weight from one powerful claw to the other. His head was tilted forward and he was looking down at us with his rust-framed eyes.

"He's right on time. When afternoon goes to the door to leave, he comes to tell it good-bye," John said cheerfully.

I tried to smile.

"You know, an owl saved my life one time," John said.

"What do you mean?"

"Remember when I was at school? The last day when we got our report cards? That was a terrible day for me."

"But you won the boys' fifty-yard dash and you were on the first-place relay team."

"Yes, but I'd failed. I'd failed that grade again. I was so sure I had passed. I had missed plenty of school—in the fall I'd worked with my family picking sugar beets . . . and then I stayed out for a month in the spring when we were thinning beets; but my dad had a job straight through the winter so I got to go to school then. The year before we had to go back up to the reservation for those months between beet harvest and planting. I tried going to the Indian school, but I was far behind when I came back to Cartersville. I wasn't surprised when I failed the year before, but to fail the same grade again. . . . I knew I wouldn't be back in school anymore after that. I was already thirteen. I couldn't stay another year in the fifth grade. I wanted to stay in school, but I couldn't go back—I was too embarrassed."

"What did your parents say?" I asked, thinking how upset my own parents would be if I left school.

"I didn't tell them. They can't read English, so they didn't know I'd failed. No one knew. I didn't tell anyone. I didn't know what I was going to do. I didn't want to just go from farm to farm working all my life like my father does. I didn't want to just sit around on the reservation. I got heavier and heavier inside. I thought I might go to work with my uncle, help him break his horses. But when I told him I wasn't going back to school, he got mad. He said if I wasn't going to school anymore, then I must be a man— I'd have to do it alone, without his help."

John stopped.

"Go on," I said, really interested now. "What did you do?"

"I didn't know what to do. I just wandered around all summer—off by myself. One day I walked way up into the sandstone cliffs. I guess I wasn't paying attention to time, and it got dark. I didn't try to find my way back. I stayed awake all night in a little hollow, just big enough for me to crouch in. In the morning I walked. I walked and watched the hawks circling. I watched their shadows on the prairie far beneath me. I saw a deer with her fawn. I wasn't hungry, but I got thirsty. I saw a draw with cedar and pine trees growing in it. I knew there must be a spring there.

"The draw ended in a steep stone hill. I began to climb. I grabbed onto rocks and sticks and branches to keep from sliding back. I got more and more thirsty. I was like an animal. Then I

heard the water running. Just a few more feet
. . . there was a shelf in the side of the hill. I had
to grasp the edge of an overhanging rock and
pull myself up. The water was there, a small pool
of water in a stone basin. As I leaned forward to
drink, I heard a noise: *Tttttttttsssssssss*. That
sound! You know it?" John's eyes were flashing.

I nodded. He had made a perfect imitation of
the sound of a rattlesnake.

"There it was—a big rattler, coiled and ready,
lying just feet away from me on the stone in
front of the water. I couldn't move. If It tried to
back up, I would have fallen over the side of the
cliff. The fear came. Strong, a lot stronger—a
million times stronger than it was with that colt
out there when the roof started to go. I could not
kill the snake. I had nothing to kill it with. There
wasn't even a rock I could reach to throw at it.
The fear was all around me. I sat very, very
still, like I had already been bitten and had died.
The snake's head rose out of the coil of its body.
Its tongue darted, forked and angry, out of its
slit mouth. I don't know how long I sat watching.
I sat like a dead man. Then the fear became still.
The hillside grew quiet. I could hear every
sound—the movement of the pine needles, the
footsteps of a chipmunk on the sandstone beneath me. There was no time. I sat. Then I
heard a strong rhythm . . . *whew, whew, whew*

. . . and an owl swept down between the branches of the pines. Bigger than I had ever seen. It landed on the stone on the other side of the basin—across from me, across from the snake.

"I watched as the owl spread its great wings out around its body. It bobbed its head up and down as it walked slowly on the edge of the pool. I didn't move. The owl jumped quickly, but I could see every move of its feathers and its talons. He struck the snake with claws and beak. The snake went stiff and rose up as if to stand on its rattlers, then it hung limp, hooked in the owl's talons, and the owl flew up and up through the pine trees and out of sight." With that, John stopped.

I could only stare at him. That was the best story I had ever heard. Daddy had told me plenty of stories when I was little, but never one like that. Tiny sliver-shivers were still running down my spine.

"That's the best story! It's incredible, fantastic!"

"You forgot all about your troubles, didn't you?" John said, grinning.

"I did . . . but it *is* a true story, isn't it? It really happened to you, didn't it? You didn't just make it up to take my mind off the colt?"

John shrugged.

The owl stirred on the branch above us. His huge brown wings, folded against his back, showed only at the edge of his white and brown breast like the lips of a giant clam shell. His head turned slowly one direction, then the other. It tilted and bobbed while his eyes examined us.

John cupped his hands over his mouth and made a strange gurgling sound. The owl tilted his head and continued to stare. John made the sound again. This time the owl lifted first one taloned foot, then the other. He moved back and forth on the branch. His head bobbed up and down very slowly, very smoothly. He repeated these motions for a moment more, then stopped and stared.

"What was he doing?" I whispered, not taking my eyes off the owl.

"He was telling me that this is his tree and these are his woods and that is his field for hunting. I can visit, but I can't get any of his mice or rabbits."

Whooo, whooo, whooo, whooo, whooo.

The deep, low, tunnel-wind sound spread through the trees and out over the pasture.

"He says it's getting dark and he has to go out hunting. He is happy we could come, but we should go home before I get in trouble," I interpreted.

"That's right. You learn fast," John said, nodding his head. "Come on," he called, crawling out of the snow house. "What should we do with this?" he asked, holding up the halter.

"I don't know. I guess I'll save it for now. Just leave it in the snow house and I'll think of what to do with it later."

As we left the cottonwoods, the owl called. His sound drifted softly through the snowflakes: *Whooo, whooo, whooo, whooo, whooo.* Somewhere way off on the other side of the river, a coyote answered with a high, wailing *ow ow ow owwwooowwwooo.*

"Good singing," John said as he took my arm to help me over a broken tree limb. "You are not going to try again with the colt?" he asked.

"No. I had my chance. I guess I can't do what I thought I could. Even with your help, there isn't enough time." I felt dull inside as I said the words.

"Where have you been, young lady?" Mom shouted the minute I opened the back door. "I called and called for you. We thought you had gone through the ice."

Before I had a chance to answer, Grandma started in on me. "Janey, I was about to send Henry out to look for you. Whatever possessed you to stay out in this weather? It's dark. We were worried half to death."

"I'm sorry I worried you. I didn't mean to. I just got to . . . doing something and I didn't pay attention to time."

There was the sound of Grandpa's footsteps stomping up the back stairs. The door opened. When he saw me, he stopped.

"Come into the kitchen, Janey. Don't stand there in the draft in your stocking feet," Grandma told me.

"No, you just stand there for a moment. I want to talk to you," Grandpa said as he came in and closed the door. He made me wait as he undid his mackinaw and took off his hat and scarf. "Well, now, that's better. It was cold out there today. Must have been cold ice skating, wasn't it?" I didn't say anything. "Janey, you have been slinking around like an egg-sucking dog since you got here. I told you I knew what you were up to and I told you to stop." He stared at me. His eyes were like black darts. "I didn't go down to see if the ice had been cleared or if there were any blade marks, but I got a feeling that you didn't ice-skate today. Did you?"

Mom and Grandma were standing back by the kitchen door. Greg was peeking his head through the curtain.

"No," I said, and tried to look him square in the eye.

"What did you do then?"

I wanted to tell him the truth . . . but I couldn't. They were making it so I couldn't tell them the truth. It was stupid. If they had just said I could try with the colt, I would have tried and found out what I had found out without all this lying and sneaking. Finally I said, "I just walked around."

"I see. Walked around in the snow—all day. By yourself?"

"No . . . with John Yellowfeather. I know him from school."

"Lenore," Grandpa blared at Mom. "Do you permit her to run around all day like that—with the help?"

"We weren't running around! We were. . . ." I couldn't tell them. I was in a trap. I had to get out. "You're just mad because he's an Indian," I said, trying to keep my voice under control.

"I wouldn't care if he was the Bonnie Prince Charlie. If he's working on the place, he's the help, and I wouldn't let you go running around in the woods with him. You little . . . you need to be knocked into line!"

"Henry, that's enough," Grandma said, trying to quiet him down.

"That's right. It's enough. You hear me, Janey. Now get up to your room, and when you come down in the morning I want you ready to toe the line for the rest of the vacation," Grandpa bellowed.

"She hasn't eaten since breakfast," Grandma said.

"I'm not hungry!" I got out of there as fast as I could.

The stove was going in the hallway, and the door to my room was open. It was warm. I climbed into bed. Alone in the dark, I started thinking about the colt again. After more than a year of hoping, planning, it was over. He would be sold. I knew there was nothing more I could do. Not without more time, not without a corral and a real hitching post. But if we had the chance . . . John and I could have done it. Grandpa was so stupid—about the colt and about John. I began to feel angry, then sad and helpless. I had to stop thinking about it. I had to think about something else. John's story . . . how strange and magical. And when the owl, our owl, appeared, it was like a fairy tale. And to-morrow was Christmas Eve. If I could get to sleep now, I would be so busy tommorrow there wouldn't be much of a chance to think about other things . . . like the colt.

The Call of the Owl

The minute I appeared in the kitchen, Grandma and Mom put me to work. They had Greg and me running up and down the stairs from breakfast until lunch. I didn't have time to feel bad about the colt. We made up all the beds, dusted the rooms, filled the lamps with kerosene, hauled wood up for the stove. Each time we finished one job, they had another waiting.

Before we knew it, Grandpa was coming in for lunch. Grandma put some leftover stew on the table and we all sat down.

"It's going to snow again," Grandpa said between bites. "I thought it had cleared for a day or two, but those clouds are building over in the northeast. Durn! Canada keeps sending us her bad weather." He was in a good mood. Grandma must have had a talk with him last night.

"I just hope it doesn't dump any more on the roads before the kids get here," Grandma worried. "Fay is due to land in Billings around eight. Ed is picking her up and they are going to drive straight here. That should put them in by two."

"It's about two hundred miles. That's about right," Grandpa said, rubbing his whiskers. "Say, Marie, while I was poking around up in the tack room this morning, I found those old harness bells. I thought I might hitch up the sled for a ride later this afternoon. Give them city dudes something special. What do you think?" Grandpa's eyes were actually twinkling as he looked at Grandma.

"That's a wonderful idea. We haven't had a sleigh ride since we worked out at that ranch near Broadus . . . twenty-five, thirty years ago."

"Well, don't tell them about it," Grandpa said, giving Greg and me a playful warning look. "I'll bring the sled down to the house sometime after they get here. We'll surprise 'em."

"This is gonna be great!" Greg shouted, clapping his hands together.

"Janey," Grandpa said as I got up to clear the table. I stopped. "I'm going to saddle up Smoky for Ed. Do you want me to throw a saddle on Blue for you, or do you want to ride in the sled?"

I thought for a moment. It would be fun to be in the sled and sit next to Aunt Fay, but maybe Uncle Ed would ride out across the river and I could go with him. He was like Grandpa. He knew about horses and he loved to ride and hunt. Whenever he could get away from his job as a mechanic at the Caterpillar tractor place in Miles City, he would come out to the ranch and take a bedroll on the back of Smoky and go out for days at a time. He slept right on the prairie, killed his food, rabbits or pheasants, and cooked it on a campfire. He was a real adventurer.

"Well . . . ?" Grandpa broke into my thoughts.

"I guess I'd like to ride Blue."

After lunch Grandma hustled around in the kitchen like a barn swallow caught in a spring wind. Mom put on a pretty wool plaid shirt and some nice slacks instead of her jeans. She was excited and happy. It made her look young and pretty. Grandma combed her hair carefully back into a bun and dabbed some rouge on her cheeks. They let Greg and me go into the living room to wait. All the stoves in the house were going, and the heat was bringing up the juices in the Christmas tree. The whole house smelled like cedar . . . like Christmas. Finally, it felt like it, too.

Maybe giving up on the colt *was* for the best, just as John had said.

"Here they come!" Greg shouted.

Uncle Ed's pickup had turned in at the gate. All of us stood at the window and watched as it moved slowly across the prairie. It took forever for it to get to the hill. When the nose of the truck poked up over the top, the horn began tooting. Aunt Fay was leaning halfway out the window on the passenger's side. Pal was going crazy, barking and jumping up on the truck. The minute it stopped, Pal rose up on his hind legs and gave Aunt Fay a lick from her chin to her forehead.

She sputtered and wiped her face with her glove. "That's my welcome, right?"

Everyone went outside, and there was lots of hugging and kissing until Grandma said, "Let's get inside. It will be snowing in a minute. Look what you brought with you." She pointed to the dark northern sky.

"We didn't bring that. Those clouds came from all the storming around you've been doing to get ready for this shindig," Uncle Ed shouted and, putting both hands around her waist, lifted her off the ground.

Grandma blushed.

"Enough of this messing around. You'd think

it was a holiday. We have work to do," Grandpa boomed.

In a few minutes, the truck was unpacked and the bags were in the proper bedrooms. There were more presents under the tree. Everyone had admired the dining room table, which Mom and Grandma had set for supper with the good china and the crystal wine glasses, and they were settling down in the kitchen where the coffeepot was perking on a crackling stove and a big plate of cookies sat in the middle of the table.

"Help yourself! Help yourself!" Grandma said to everyone.

Grandpa went into his bedroom and came back with a bottle of whiskey. He poured some for my uncle and some for himself. Grandma frowned at him. Aunt Fay laughed. She looked so pretty.

"You look wonderful," Grandma said and hugged her, "but I hope you didn't wear those blue jeans on the airplane."

"Mother, you are incorrigibly, delightfully old-fashioned . . . about dress as well as about Dad's nips. Of course I did. You weren't going to catch me coming out to the ranch looking like a dude. I figured I'd have to take enough abuse from the old man as it is. I haven't been on a horse for two years."

I laughed.

She spun around. "And what are you giggling about? Just look at you." She took me by the shoulders and turned me around. "Mmmmmm. You are taller, much taller than I imagined. I wonder if Santy brought you the right size. Well, I can't help it. That's your fault for growing so much . . . or your mother's for feeding you too well . . . or your father's for giving you those big Swedish genes."

Aunt Fay was funny, just the way I remembered her, but even better. She treated me differently . . . more like a friend. She asked me about school and my friends. I could tell she was really interested.

There was a pause in the talking and laughing. Aunt Fay suddenly held up her hand: "Listen! What's that?"

Into the stillness, came a sound like a thousand spoons tapping on fancy glasses. Aunt Fay ran over to the kitchen window. "It's unbelievable! Come here!"

We all crowded in at the big window. Grandpa was in the weathered gray sled driving the matched black team across the flat white yard. The gray barn and corrals blended into the clouds, and giant feather snowflakes were falling over it all.

"Well, I'll be. . . . How did he sneak out of here to do that!" Uncle Ed exclaimed.

"They will never believe this in Chicago," Aunt Fay said, shaking her head.

I was standing close to Grandma. I reached out and took her hand. She squeezed it tightly. I looked up and saw there were wet places in the corners of her eyes. She was smiling at the scene, at everything. Her gray hair matched the window frost. The wrinkles in her cheeks and around her eyes were every which way, like the delicate cracks that spread across the morning skin of ice on the water pail when you press your finger against it. She was glowing, just like the winter light outside.

I stayed with her at the window when the others went to put on their coats.

"We'd better get out there. We don't want to be left behind," she said finally, wiping at her eyes with her apron as though she had gotten some flour or a piece of wood ash in them.

When we appeared on the porch, Grandpa said, "Come on. I got the horse saddled so you can ride escort."

Blue was tied to the back of the sled. Uncle Ed was fastening his rifle scabbard on Smoky's saddle. The dogs started barking and ran toward the hill. In a moment our pickup truck appeared. Daddy was here in time for the sleigh ride. He drove right up to the sled and stopped the pickup. In a moment he was out and sitting on the back of the sled, his legs dangling over the side. I was glad to see him. His dark blue overcoat was sprinkled with snowflakes and hay. The fur flaps of his hat fell down over his cheeks. He loved storybook things like this on the ranch. He was laughing as Grandpa shouted, "We're off," and the sled jerked forward.

The harness bells jingled and tinkled as the sled runners hissed through the snow. Greg giggled and threw armfuls of hay into the air so it showered down on everyone. Then Aunt Fay's voice rose up from the sleigh and floated into the afternoon with the snowflakes:

"Jingle bells, jingle bells. . . ." she sang.

We all joined in. Next came "Over the river and through the woods, to Grandmother's house we go. The horse knows the way to carry the sleigh over the drifted snowoo."

The dogs jumped a rabbit and went barking after it in their own kind of song. Grandpa motioned me over to the sled.

"Ain't this something," he said. His eyebrows were thick with snowflakes. "But you know what I did? I got that little silver flask ready to go and I left it in the the washroom . . . on the shelf by the water pail. I could certainly use a nip to warm myself, and I bet the others could, too. Would you go back and get it for me? Don't tell your grandmother what you're doing." He winked. He really wasn't mad anymore.

"Will do," I said, and turned Blue around before anybody on the sled noticed.

Blue was his fastest going back to the barn. We arrived quickly, and I found the flask right where Grandpa said he had left it. I was mounting up again when I saw John coming down from the bunkhouse with a pail.

"Merry Christmas!" I shouted. He waved back. I rode over and waited for him at the pump.

"Did you see everyone in the sled? It was Grandpa's idea to have a sleigh ride. It's fun. Hey, hop on and come back with me. My dad's there. I want you to meet him."

John shook his head.

"Come on," I pleaded, really wanting him along. "We won't be down there much longer. I'm just riding along behind the sled. Come on."

"I better not."

"Please. It's Christmas Eve. . . ."

"Well, OK."

He climbed up on Blue. I tapped the horse with the reins, and we took off. An off-key version of "Away in a Manger" drifted out from the sled. John groaned and covered his ears.

"Hey, Grandpa!" I called as we drew near the sled.

"It took you long. . . ." He stopped short when he saw John.

I handed him the flask, holding my breath.

"Henry!" Grandma exclaimed from the sled (struggling to be heard above ". . . laid down his sweet head. . . ."). "Did you send her all the way up to the house for that?"

"Come on, Mom," Uncle Ed yelled. "Don't be such a WCTUer."

"What's a double-you-see-tea-you-are?" Greg asked.

"It's a little old lady in a long black dress with a skinny, pinched-up face who goes around breaking bottles of Christmas cheer," Uncle Ed answered him.

"And a Christmas cheer to that!" said Aunt Fay. "Hip, hip. . . ."

"Hooray!" Greg shouted at the top of his lungs.

During the silliness I dropped back to the rear of the sled. No one else had noticed John.

Then Aunt Fay leaned out of the sled. She squinted into the gathering twilight and snow.

"Who's your friend, Janey?"

It became very quiet. At least I thought so, but my heart was pounding so loudly, maybe I just couldn't hear outside myself. "This is John Yellowfeather," I answered as calmly as I could.

"Pleased to meet you, John. Do you live near the ranch?" Aunt Fay asked.

I wished she would shut up.

Before John could answer, Grandpa said in a

loud voice, "This is a family celebration, Janey. Take your friend home and get yourself back down here."

"Henry!" Grandma said just as loudly.

I was messing this up for her . . . for John. The sled runners made a *ssshhhsing* sound. The harness bells jingled.

Daddy was gripping the edge of the sled with both hands. He smiled at me, but his smile was stiff.

"I'm pleased you have invited John," Daddy said. "I see no reason why he shouldn't be along on this sleigh ride."

"Let's get warmed up again," Mom said, and she started singing "Hark the Herald Angels Sing." Her voice was chokey, but Grandma and Aunt Fay joined in immediately so you hardly noticed it.

"If I'm going to get a shot at a rabbit I'd better get going," Uncle Ed said. He ticked Smoky with his heels and rode off to the cottonwoods.

"We're coming with you, Uncle Ed," I called. I had to get away from the sled. I didn't know what Grandpa would do next.

"I'm sorry, so sorry," I whispered to John when we got away from them. "I know. . . . I know you think he doesn't want you there because you're an Indian. I thought that yesterday when he was mad at me for being out so long

143

with you; but he said that wasn't true. He said he doesn't like me 'running with the help.' I know that is silly, real old-fashioned but. . . ." John was silent. "You don't believe that, do you?"

"I believe it . . . maybe . . . I don't know. . . . My father says your grandpa is pretty tough, but that he doesn't treat him bad . . . doesn't insult him. But *you* are my friend, not your grandpa," John said suddenly with anger. "My mother doesn't want me to be with you, either. She says things about you. They are the way they are. It's just the way things are." He slapped his glove against the back of the saddle in angry emphasis.

Blue had slowed to a walk, and Uncle Ed was ahead of us as we entered the cottonwoods. John leaned forward and gripped my arm. "Look over there," he whispered.

Overhead, above the snarled branches, sliding silently on outspread wings, was the owl. Down, down through the falling snow he came. Through the branches with tilting wingtips. Sliding, never touching. He landed on his perch. He settled himself with a big *whoosh* of his wings.

Whooo, whooo, whooo, whooo, whooo. His call came as a greeting.

"He sounds better than your relatives," John said.

"He's probably nicer, too."

Crrack! A branch snapped near us. I looked toward the sound. Uncle Ed and Smoky had ridden up. They were quite close, but they didn't see us. I waved to Uncle Ed. He saw me and nodded a greeting, then motioned for me to be quiet. He was adjusting the sight on his rifle. He lifted it to his shoulder and placed his cheek against the stock. I watched him raise the barrel. He steadied it upward.

"Oh, no!" I tried to shout, but no sound would come. John saw, too. He kicked Blue and the horse jumped forward. The shock of the movement brought me to my senses. I turned Blue toward Uncle Ed. Blue covered the short distance in seconds, but it seemed like years.

"No!" I shouted as Blue came in so close to Smoky that my stirrup caught Uncle Ed's. "No!" I yelled again. I reached out and tried to grab the barrel of his rifle. There was a thunderous bang as the gun went off. I threw my hands over my face, dropping my reins. Blue stopped. My shoulders shook, my legs trembled. I didn't uncover my eyes.

"Are you losing your mind, Janey? Why did you do that?" Uncle Ed stormed, his voice heavy with anger.

John was holding my elbow gently. Then he squeezed. I heard the familiar *whoosh* as the wings lifted the owl up. Up and out of sight above the snowy trees. There was no time for Uncle Ed to get another shot. I dropped my hands. Uncle Ed looked at me and shook his head in disgust. He blew out a steamy breath as he put his rifle back in its scabbard. He looked at me and started to say something, then shook his head and jerked on Smoky's reins. John and I watched him leave the cottonwoods. We could hear the harness bells as the sled rounded the corner of the pasture.

John got down off the horse and picked up the reins, which were dangling in the snow. He handed them to me and climbed back on Blue. I started us off through the trees where we wouldn't meet up with the sled. We didn't talk. I was too worried. I'd messed the day up good. I wondered what Uncle Ed was telling everyone. But I had no choice. I couldn't let him shoot the owl. How could I get them to understand that?

When we reached the barn we dismounted, and I put Blue inside. I could hear the bells below the hill. They would be up here soon. John was gone.

When the sled pulled up to the back porch, I was already out of my coat and sitting in the dark in the kitchen. As the jingle of the bells started up again, the back door opened, and I heard Aunt Fay:

"I understand why she did it. Ed's being silly.

He should understand. Why should he shoot the owl anyway? It isn't getting any chickens in the dead of winter. As for Dad's being upset about her little friend. Ridiculous! I learned a long time ago about the old man. I love him, but you have to watch out for him. If he likes you when you're little, he builds you up, gets you to develop just the characteristics that he hates in you as you get older . . . independence, strength. . . ."

Grandma said, "Well, it's over now, and when she comes in we are going to act as if everything is hunky-dory. Nothing at all about this. It's done!" She walked into the kitchen and fumbled for matches at the stove. In a moment she had a lamp lit and saw me sitting there.

Before I said a word she called to Mom and Aunt Fay, "Janey is here already."

They both came into the room. "Good! Then she heard what I said and I won't have to repeat it." Aunt Fay laughed.

Grandma put all of us to work lighting lamps, filling relish dishes, hunting up the serving platter for the roast beef. Everything was just as planned.

There was shuffling and scuffling on the back porch as the men returned from putting up the horses. Now I had to face Grandpa and Uncle Ed. Suddenly Aunt Fay was right beside me with her arm around my shoulders. "I can't wait for you to open one of the presents I brought. I hope it fits. You really are much bigger than I had thought . . . and I don't mean only in size. Stick to your guns and don't back down!" she said, as all the men trooped into the kitchen.

Grandma lost no time herding us all into the dining room. Aunt Fay saw that I was seated by her. She had brought wine for dinner. She rose, and poured it all around. When everyone had some, she called on the "creator of the feast" to propose a toast. We applauded as Grandma stood up.

"I thank the powers that we are all here together one more time. . . ." Glasses were raised to drink.

It was a real celebration. Aunt Fay poured lots of wine.

When we finished our pie, Grandpa suggested we have coffee in the living room around the tree. He got out his brandy from the liquor chest beside the library table. He poured shot glasses for Uncle Ed and himself. He was about to propose a toast before he remembered Daddy.

Aunt Fay complained. "You're mighty forgetful. I'll have some of that, too. And don't pull any of that let-the-men-drink-because-it-puts-hair-on-their-chest stuff with me."

Grandpa poured her a glass with a fake look of disgust. Everyone started telling stories, but they were about Mom's family and Daddy was left out. Before long, he excused himself, saying he needed to go and take a walk after that big dinner. I followed him to the washroom.

"Can I come with you?"

"No, you stay and enjoy the party."

"I'd rather go with you. They don't need me."

"I'm proud of you, Janey," Daddy said as he fastened his overcoat.

"Why?"

"I'm proud of the courage and intelligence you are showing. That's all."

"I'm coming with you."

Daddy and I stepped out into the snow. Everything was changed into something else by the rapidly falling flakes. The lilac bushes by the dining room windows had become fat people wrapped in ghost sheets for Halloween. The round horse trough out by the pump was a cake covered with Grandma's fluffy boiled frosting. There was no moon or stars, but the light coming through the windows grew bigger in the snow. It seemed to slide and spread on the whiteness.

"That reminds me," Daddy said. "I've got a good lantern in the pickup."

We walked out to the truck. As he opened the door to get the lantern from behind the seat, I saw a box sitting there. It was a plain grocery box, but it was tied with a red ribbon.

"What's that?"

"It's a ham, a fruitcake and a few other things for the Yellowfeathers. Maybe I should take it up there now. It's very cold out here, and it might freeze." He lifted the box out and gave me the lantern. We walked up to the bunkhouse.

A light shone from the window. We could hear voices speaking in Cheyenne as we mounted the steps. I knocked. Tom Yellowfeather's tall frame appeared in the doorway.

"Merry Christmas, Tom," Daddy said. "How are things?"

"Pretty good," Mr. Yellowfeather said.

I tried to see into the room to find John, but I couldn't without being conspicuous.

"I got a little something here for Christmas dinner," Daddy said, handing him the box. Mr. Yellowfeather thanked him.

"I'm glad to hear things are OK. My daughter says you have a fine boy there, too," Daddy said.

Mr. Yellowfeather nodded and smiled. Daddy waved to him, and went down the steps as Mr. Yellowfeather closed the door.

"He's a good hand. I've never heard a complaint about him in the valley. I would like to keep him on here if he can get along with your grandfather."

"Daddy, are you paying him the same amount of money you would pay Jim Gordon?"

"I'm paying him what he asked for," Daddy answered.

"But is it the same?"

"No. No, it isn't."

"Why not?"

"Because he asked for less. . . ."

"Why?" I was angry. I knew I was making Daddy feel bad, and I didn't care. He was always telling me about justice and equality! I would have stuck up for him to the very end with Grandpa and Grandma. I would never have believed them about the money situation and the help. Now here he was admitting they were right.

"Janey, I know it's not right, but he gets paid less because it's harder for him to find work, steady work at least, because he is Cheyenne."

"But you said he did good work. You said. . . ."

"I know. It isn't right!"

"Daddy, he has a family to support and you pay him less than you do Jim Gordon who is all alone . . . and for the same work!"

"Oh, God, it's a mess. I know. Janey, you are right to call me on this. I've been looking at everything in terms of money. I got so worried when I had that heart attack, I tried to put every cent I could into the place in case I had to retire from the railroad right away, in case the ranch suddenly became our sole support. But you're right. I can't retire on that fifteen dollars a month I'm not paying him. But it could make him feel a lot better."

Whooo, whooo, whooo, whooo, whooo. That long call dangled over us in the snowy air on the edge of the pasture.

Daddy and I both stopped. "Do you think that's your friend?" he asked me.

"I'm sure it is. Come and see him," I said, grabbing Daddy's hand and pulling him off the pasture path on which we had been walking and into the trees.

I went straight to the tree where the owl usually perched, the first place we had seen him. He wasn't there. He hooted again from down closer to the river. We picked our way through the trees. When we reached the willows at the river's edge, the owl sounded again. He was close by. I swung the light up into the trees.

"There he is!" I whispered to Daddy.

The owl sat on a low branch which hung over the willows and stretched out over the river. His wings were arced and held away from his body as though he wore a great feathered cape.

Daddy gasped, "How beautiful! How beautiful!"

The owl slowly turned his head. The beam from the lantern caught his eyes, and they lit up like the candles on the Christmas tree. Daddy and I both drew a quick breath. Then, opening his great wings further, the owl pushed off the snowy branch and was gone in the darkness.

Suddenly there was a groaning, grumbling sound, then a splashing. A horse whinnied. There was more splashing. Daddy and I tried to see through the willows. We ran closer to the riverbank, the frozen willow branches tearing at our coats. The splashing grew louder! As we came through the willows and out onto the river bank, I shined the light onto the ice. Thrashing and fighting, struggling to lift himself from the freezing water, was the colt.

"Good Lord!" Daddy exclaimed. "Hold that light steady! What's happened here?"

I tried to focus the beam from the lantern. My hands were shaking. About midriver, the colt had gone through the ice. The water wasn't deep, just up over his knees it appeared, but he was terrified. The water, the icy water, swirled around his legs as he reared and struggled to escape.

"Run to the house! Get ropes and horses!" Daddy shouted to me.

I shook my head, "You go! Go! I'll stay!"

"You keep the light on him and signal us with it when we get down here. We've got to get him out right away." Daddy was gone.

There was more splashing. I looked at the hole. The colt had reached forward with his foot.

He lifted it up on the ice edge. It slipped back into the water. He stumbled and went down on his front knees, his chest in the freezing wetness. He struggled to stand. His back legs slid to the side. He almost went down again. I remembered the stallion, the colt's father, standing in the river with the spirit draining out of him. That wasn't going to happen to the colt. If only I could calm him. The water wasn't deep, but he was going to cut himself on the ice, or slip and fall. I shuddered. I had to do something. Holding the lantern steady on him, I walked farther out onto the ice. It groaned beneath me. I stopped. All was quiet except for the muffled sound of running water. The beam of light from the lantern penetrated the darkness and fell on the colt. His winter coat was matted with snow so that he was white, too, framed by the black hole in the ice.

I felt dizzy, and swallowed hard as I looked at him standing in the water.

"This is a fine state of affairs. Here we are out in a snowstorm all alone on Christmas Eve. And you're standing in icy water. You must be pretty cold. Don't you worry, though. We're going to have you out of that hole before you can say 'Jack Robinson,' " I said, imitating Grandma. "You are not going to have the stuffing knocked out of you by that old river. Nope. Not like your father. I knew your father. He was the most beautiful horse in the world. You look just like him. Do you hear me?" I called out to him, close to tears once more. I stopped talking for a moment.

Then I remembered stories I had read about people freezing to death. They always went to sleep first.

"Now you listen to me and stay awake. We're going to get you out. Then we'll rub you down and warm you up. You stay awake."

I continued talking. I didn't know what else I could do. The colt answered with a snorty sound.

"You're lucky this river isn't very deep in the winter. How did you fall through, anyway? The ice is thick. Grandpa crosses it with Smoky. Smoky weighs more than you do."

I was running out of things to talk about. Why didn't they come? Daddy hadn't been gone long, but it seemed like hours. It was so quiet when I stopped talking. I began to sing.

"Silent night, holy night. . . ."

The colt shifted in the icy water.

"Stop that jumping around!" I said. "We'll have you out of there in a minute. Just calm down."

The colt threw his head back and tried to back away from me. I wasn't helping. I took a few more steps toward the hole. The ice cracked. I stood very still. The colt was twisting from side to side. His back legs gave way again, and his haunches slid into the water. His eyes rolled, white, blank.

"Oh, why don't they get here?" I whispered. How could I get him to settle down? I remembered that first day John put the halter on him, how still he had become when John made that humming sound. I tried to imitate it. Nothing happened, but he probably couldn't hear me over the sound of the swift current and his splashing. I tried to get closer. I moved across the ice inch by inch, stopping when it groaned or cracked, then moving forward toward the colt, humming. Humming as loudly as I could, my lips pressed together, the sound coming out from deep in my chest. The colt grew more quiet. He stood quite still in the water. I hummed, stopping only to get my breath. The snow fell on the colt. The water rushed between his legs.

"Janey!"

I turned the light to the call. John appeared carrying the halter and a lariat.

"The others are saddling the horses. What is the ice like near the hole?" John asked me as he walked out onto it with no hesitation. I couldn't answer him, but he was examining it already.

"I think we can walk him out of this, but we have to do it right away. Horses' legs. . . ." He stopped talking and handed me the halter. "You are going to have to get his on him. I'll throw a rope on him and try to hold him for you if he starts acting up, but you have to get the halter on because you wouldn't be able to hold him for me." John made a loop in the lariat and deftly tossed it over the colt's head. When he pulled up on it, the colt reared. John held him.

"Now get over there and put that on him. You might have to get wet, but go ahead. We have to get him out, fast."

I moved closer to the hole. "Come on. This is your big chance to show us how much you've learned. Just let me get you out of that hole. Let me lead you out of here before your legs freeze." The colt snorted. He shook snow from his mane. I was on the edge of the hole. I began the humming again. I stepped forward and reached out and touched his nose. He didn't move. I pulled the halter on his nose, humming, stretching out over the hole. I couldn't reach up over his ears. John saw this. He tried giving the lariat a little pull. The colt lurched backward against it. Now I couldn't reach him. I leaned farther out over the hole. As I looked down, my stomach flopped over. The water was black and silver as it swirled beneath me. I knew what I had to do. I stepped down. I felt the current swirl and push at my legs as I waded, struggling to get next to the colt. He shivered all over. If he reared, if he kicked, we might both go down. "Please, please. Don't move now. Help me. Help us. Save us. Don't move." I kept humming, trying to be heard above the rushing water. I reached out and patted his shoulder. He stood. I stepped forward and did it! Suddenly I had the halter over his ears and fastened . . . like magic.

John saw it happen. "Good. Now get out of there and lead him up to the edge of the hole," he called.

In a moment, I had lifted myself up onto the edge. My boots were filled with water, but I had no time to think about it. John was beside me.

"Lead him. When he is close to the edge, I'll help him lift his hooves up into the snow where he can get a grip."

I walked toward the bank, gently pulling on the lead rope. The colt followed! When he was right up to the ice, John reached down and helped him lift his hoof up. He guided it into the snow. The other foot followed. I moved ahead with the lead.

The colt put his weight on his front legs. He leaned forward. If only the ice was strong enough. If only it would hold. He was almost out. I pulled forward again. One back leg came up out of the water. It touched the ice at the edge of the hole, but slipped back in again.

"Come on, boy." I could feel the tears choking up in my throat. "Move. You've been in that water too long."

The owl called.

"Come on, you cayuse! Even that old bird wants you out of this mess," John said.

The colt lifted his back leg again. This time the hoof hit the edge of the ice and stayed there. I moved ahead. The colt lifted the other foot. He was out! I swallowed my shouts and kept coaxing him forward. We had to take him out of danger, farther from the hole. He allowed us to lead him all the way up on the bank.

There was a commotion in the cottonwoods as Uncle Ed and Tom Yellowfeather rode up on Smoky and Blue. The lantern still shone on the empty hole in the ice.

"Looks like we're late. I surely don't mind. I was afraid we'd find that little red fella standing on four icicles instead of legs," Uncle Ed said as he dismounted.

"How long was he in there?" Tom Yellowfeather asked John.

"Didn't take us long to get him out. I don't know how long he was there before they found him, though," John answered.

"We heard him fall in . . . he wasn't there too long."

I prayed he wasn't there too long.

"Sounds like he might be all right. We better get him walking. Get his circulation going," Tom Yellowfeather said. "You know, these horses can take a lot. They can stand in a drift with their backs to the wind during a daylong blizzard and be just fine."

There was the sound of horses and the swish of the sled runners in the snow.

"Here comes the old man with the sled. Luckily, we won't be needing to haul anything," Uncle Ed said. "Janey, you get started, lead him on up to the barn."

I looked back at the colt. He stood in the snow, head down, hanging, so defeated, looking so much like the stallion. I gave a pull on the rope, and the colt moved with me. There was no resistance. The sled pulled up beside me. Daddy was on the seat beside Grandpa.

"He's out," Uncle Ed called to them, "but we got to get him up to the barn and work on him. Janey's going to lead him. Keep an eye on her. I'm going to ride ahead and get the kerosene stove going in that milk room." Uncle Ed galloped off.

Daddy climbed down from the sled to walk with me. The colt followed with no fight. He looked awful. His coat was full of snow. His mane had ice balls dangling from it. It wasn't over yet.

Daddy reached for my hand and held it tightly.

"Please let him stay alive. Please let his legs not be frozen. Don't make him lame. . . ." I felt Pal gently rub against me. Someone touched my other hand, and I looked over. John walked with us on the other side of the colt.

Harmony

Tom Yellowfeather held the barn door open. Uncle Ed took the lead rope from me.

"Go down and get some hot water and blankets from your grandmother, Janey, and get warmed up yourself," he told me.

John and Daddy went into the barn, and I ran to the house. I was out of breath as I burst into the kitchen. Mom, Grandma, and Aunt Fay were sitting around the table. Greg had fallen asleep on the floor.

"Did they get him out? How is he?" They all spoke at once.

"He's up in the barn. They don't know how he is yet. His legs might be hurt from standing in the water." My throat caught on the words. I coughed hard and went on, "We need blankets and hot water, right away."

Grandma was up from the table, putting a pan of water on the stove. Then she went to their bedroom and returned carrying a pile of old blankets.

Mom took off my hat and smoothed my hair. Then she saw my wet jeans and boots. "Janey! Get out of those wet things right now. You must be frozen yourself. Sit down. One of us will take those back up to the barn. You must stay here and get warm."

"I can't! I have to go back!" I shouted.

"You're hysterical, too. You need to rest," she said, trying to calm me.

"No! I'm going back. I have to!" I burst into tears. Aunt Fay came over and hugged me. I tried to control my crying. "I have to go back, Mom. He needs me. He might die."

"He's made it this far, Janey. I'll bet he can go the rest of the distance. You get out of those wet things and into something dry." Mom spoke so calmly and sympathetically I was stunned.

"I'll go back up there with her. All right, Lenore?" Aunt Fay said.

Mom nodded.

I ran upstairs and got dry clothes right away. Aunt Fay put on her coat and we went out carrying the blankets, two teakettles of hot water and a pot of coffee. Grandma stuffed two tin cups in my coat pockets.

The milk room was lit by a gas lantern hanging from a hook on the wall. There was a small, round kerosene heater in the corner. Uncle Ed and Tom Yellowfeather were in the hay on the floor, examining the colt's legs.

"It's hard to say, but I think he's going to be OK. Sure doesn't have any spunk, though."

"Looks like he's in some kind of shock," Grandpa said. "I say wrap his legs and give him a good rubdown."

"Let's try it, anyway," Ed said. He tossed a gunny sack to Tom Yellowfeather from a pile in the corner. They wrapped the colt's legs loosely in the sacks and tied them with twine. Then they each took a sack and began to rub the colt all over in brisk, circular strokes.

"We'll work in shifts," Uncle Ed said. He looked over at me. "You and John have done your share, Janey. You don't have to do this, too."

"I want to."

Uncle Ed only nodded as he rubbed. The room was quiet except for the hissing of the gas lantern and the sound of the rough gunny sack on the colt's hide. That stopped. "Next shift," Uncle Ed said.

John and Daddy took over. Tom Yellowfeather and Uncle Ed went over by the heater. Grandpa poured them a cup of coffee. I watched as Grandpa handed them each a cup.

"Beats me how he fell through," Ed said. "The ice was thick enough around the hole."

Grandpa stared down at the floor for a moment. He reached inside his mackinaw and pulled out his sack of Bull Durham. Then he spoke: "That was an old water hole. I chopped a new one a few days back. Misjudged the weather. Didn't think it was going to mess around and snow. I thought it was going to be dry-bone cold and that old hole would freeze thicker than a cottonwood log overnight. Didn't get cold enough. I should have chopped that hole open again." He shook his head sadly and looked at the colt.

He banged his coffee cup down on the kerosene stove. "I know, I'm going to make up a little oat mash. Maybe I'll throw in a shot of whiskey. That ought to get him up on all fours again," Grandpa said quickly.

"Or knock him off them. You drink strong stuff!" Ed joked quietly. Tom Yellowfeather grinned and sipped his coffee. Daddy and John finished their shift.

"You and Fay ready?" Uncle Ed asked me. I nodded. He handed us our gunny sacks and we went to work.

I leaned by weight into my arms to make the rubbing heavy, to make it move through the colt's winter coat, through his skin, into his muscles.

Grandpa returned with the mash bucket and set it down beside the stove to warm up. He picked up a coffee cup and poured it full from the pot on the heater. As he sipped, he turned toward Tom Yellowfeather. "How did you get him out of that hole, anyway?" he asked.

"We didn't. When we got there, your granddaughter and John had him up on the bank already."

Grandpa turned to John. "How did you do it?" he asked.

I kept on rubbing. John was talking to Grandpa, but his voice was so low I couldn't hear what he was saying. What would he tell him? Would he tell him about sneaking down and trying to get the colt on lead? For a moment, I panicked. Grandpa would know about my lies . . . but it didn't matter now. If the colt lived because we were able to get him out on lead, it didn't matter. I looked at the colt. He showed little resemblance now to that kicking, rearing creature that had almost ripped down the horse shed. I rubbed harder. Words began to join the movement of my arms. "Run, run, run, kick, kick, rear, rear, fly, fly." My arms moved faster, faster.

"Time," Uncle Ed said.

He and Tom Yellowfeather took over again. I walked over to Daddy and John. Aunt Fay joined us.

"Here, drink this," she said, thrusting a hot cup of coffee into my hands.

"No, I don't drink coffee."

"Take it. You want to stay awake, don't you?"

Daddy frowned as I took a sip. "*Aaaaackkk!*" I spit the bitter-tasting stuff on the floor. Aunt Fay burst out laughing.

Just then the colt lifted his head and shook his mane, as though he were just waking up.

"Look, look at the colt!" I shouted.

"By golly, he's picking up a little," Daddy said.

He *was* picking up! He tossed his head again. When Aunt Fay moved closer to get a look, he turned and nudged her with his nose.

"Bring the blankets," Uncle Ed said. "Wrap him up! Where is that mash bucket?"

They tossed the blankets over his back. Grandma's old blankets were so full of holes, they had to put blankets over the holes.

"Ain't that just like the old lady," Grandpa snorted.

Ed stuck the mash bucket under the colt's nose. He sniffed it once or twice, then dipped down in and slurped a mouthful.

The milk room was instantly filled with excitement. Grandpa and Tom Yellowfeather were grinning and talking over their coffee cups. Daddy was watching Uncle Ed coaxing the colt to take more mash, as Aunt Fay stroked his neck. John and I were just watching everybody. I felt so good. For this moment, everything was right.

Grandpa looked over. He stared at John and me for a few seconds, then he went over to Daddy. They were whispering and nodding. "If it's all right with you . . . ?" Grandpa said out loud.

Daddy was leaning against the wall. He looked down at the floor. He rubbed his chin and kicked at the hay. Then he looked up at Grandpa. "It's no solution, Henry," he said quietly.

"No, but it's important. And some of the money for the mares can help on the hay."

Daddy shrugged. Finally, he nodded.

"It'll be fine," Grandpa declared. "He's going to be fine, but he'll need someone to take special care of him for a week or so. He's a tough hunk of horseflesh. Stubborn! He's got his own mind. But then, so has she. I think it's a fair match."

I looked at the colt draped in the tattered blankets, his muzzle stuck into the mash bucket. I looked at Aunt Fay. She was grinning from one ear to the other. I thought I understood what Grandpa was saying, but. . . .

"Merry Christmas, Janey," he said softly.

"Merry Christmas!" everyone echoed.

I couldn't speak, so I smiled . . . the biggest smile I could find from deep down inside me. I turned to John. "His name is Rekker," I whispered.

The colt slurped very loudly.

"Now, it's your job to teach him some manners," Grandpa said, amidst the laughter.

And somewhere down below the barn, I thought I heard the owl.

About the Author

June Andrea Hanson was born in Miles City,
Montana and grew up on a ranch nearby. She
graduated from the University of Colorado and
spent two years in the Peace Corps. Currently,
she lives with her two daughters in New York
City where she is a practicing psycho-physio-
therapist and part-time writer. *Winter of the Owl*
is Ms. Hanson's second novel.